A Raccoon's Tale
Seven Saves the Notch

A Raccoon's Tale
Seven Saves the Notch

Fran Hodgkins

Illustrated by Donnachada Daly

BRATTLE
PUBLISHING GROUP

 Published by Brattle Publishing Group, LLC.
www.brattlepublishing.com

Book Design by Bumblecat Design and Illustration
Illustrations by Donnachada Daly
Cover Illustration by Samuel Valentino

Brattle Publishing Group
Attention: Permissions
4546 Westway Ave.
Dallas, TX 75205

ISBN 13: 978-0-9908706-3-0
ISBN 10: 0990870634

Printed in the United States of America
First edition, March 2016

For Win, Ros, and Tess

Chapter 1

"Wake up, sleepyhead."

Seven-Rings twitched her left ear, opened her eyes, and looked up into her mother's face. Runner Moon's eyes glowed with love as she gazed back at her kit.

"Have you gone out yet, Mama?" Seven asked.

"I did. I brought breakfast!" She held out a small parcel wrapped in yellow paper.

"Amburger!" cried Typhoo, Seven's brother, suddenly wide awake and in full spring. He grabbed at the package, hissing, "Mine!"

"Not yours!" said Seven-Rings as she ripped the package in half. "We all share!"

The movement woke the littlest kit, Arnica, who blinked and yawned. She gazed at the dappled light pouring through the former Ladies' Group parlor of the abandoned church that the raccoon family called home. Seven handed part of the treat to her sister. "Here, Arni. Breakfast."

Arnica took her portion of the burger and bit and chewed it slowly. Seven-Rings loved Arnica, even more than she loved their boisterous brother. Yet Arni was so different. She could spend hours just watching motes of dust float in a sunbeam.

Runner said, "You are so good to her, Seven."

"Mama, why is Arnica so, well, different from Typhoo and me?" Seven asked.

Runner licked her smallest kit's face. Arni licked her back. "Her birth and first days were difficult. She was not as strong as you or Typhoo, and she needed more help. But each of us is different. It's enough that Arnica is her own sweet self, isn't it?"

Typhoo was watching Seven hungrily, his eyes glittering. "It's mine, greedy," she said, and stuffed the piece of hamburger into her mouth.

"Typhoo, play with Arni," Runner Moon ordered. "Seven, come with me."

Typhoo said, "Come on, Arni! Let's play Acorn!"

They sat down and began rolling an ancient acorn across the worn wooden floor. Having long ago lost its cap, the acorn rolled in a straight line, making it ideal for playing catch.

Runner and Seven-Rings left behind the former Ladies'

Group parlor and headed to the sanctuary. The building, with its broken windows that let in the spring breeze, stood at the end of a block, surrounded by a weedy lot that had once been a splendid garden.

The Moon family—Seven's grandmother as well as her great-aunt and her six kits—had moved in not long after the people had stopped coming to the church and it had closed. But they were all gone, and now Seven, Runner, Typhoo, and Arni were the only Moon family members that lived in the church.

They were not alone. Seven's family shared the space with the rats in the watery basement and the bats that lived in the rafters of the sanctuary and flew in and out through the triangular windows in the roof.

Seven knew to avoid the basement, but she did creep out on the rafters now and then to listen to the bats' sweet high voices. Yet today they sounded different somehow.

Runner climbed up the standpipe and crept through a hole that led out to the rafters. Seven, too, scrambled up the pipe and caught the edge of the hole where it entered the wall. Peeking through the hole, she spotted her mother on one of the wide rafters, deep in conversation with the largest bat in the colony. The air behind them was a blur of wings. The bats were on the move, every single one of them, even the grizzled elders and the expectant mothers.

"You must leave now," Seven-Rings heard the bat say.

Suddenly the building shook as if struck by lightning. Seven-Rings lost her grip and tumbled backwards.

Her mother appeared at her side. "We have to get Typhoo and Arnica and get out, now!" Seven scrambled to her paws, and they raced back toward the ladies' parlor.

Typhoo was screaming in fear. Inside the parlor, a huge chunk of the roof and part of the wall behind the sofa had vanished. Outside, visible through the hole where the wall had been, stood a giant yellow monster with jaws full of rubble. "Mama!" cried Typhoo. "It's eating our house!"

Seven-Rings clung to the doorjamb, frozen by the sight of the monster as it opened its jaws and let the pieces fall to the ground. Arnica stood in the middle of the floor, holding the acorn and staring. Typhoo stood on the couch, back arched and fur puffed out. He did his best to scare the monster away, but it took no notice. It turned its head and clamped its massive jaws onto the wall above the sofa. With a roar, it tore the wall loose.

Runner grabbed Arnica and threw her toward the doorway. The sight of her sister flying at her broke Seven's daze. She caught Arnica and together they rolled out into the hallway. "Run!" their mother cried.

Seven dragged Arnica away from the ladies' parlor and down a flight of stairs. The building shuddered. "Come on, Arni," Seven gasped.

"But . . . Mama . . . Typhoo . . ." Arni slipped from Seven-Rings's grasp and started back up the stairs.

"No!" Seven cried. She grabbed Arni's tail.

"Ow! What'd you do that for?" Arni said crossly.

Seven took a deep breath, knowing how important it was not to frighten her sister into freezing. "Mama wants us to go this way."

"Mama!" Arnica called up the stairwell. The only answer was a grinding roar from above.

Seven shut her eyes as the old church shook again. Far above, she heard the voices of the bats heightened with fright as the stragglers hurried to escape from the creaking, groaning rafters. Keeping her voice steady and light, she said, "Come with me, Arni. It's going to be OK."

Although it took a terrifyingly long time, she got Arnica downstairs and out through the broken panel in the side door. The sunshine streamed down, warming the flowers that grew in the abandoned alley and filling the air with their fragrance. Seven-Rings pinned her ears back at the roar that came from the other side of the building.

"Get outta the way!" snarled a voice behind them. Seven-Rings pulled Arnica aside. A large group of rats clambered out through the hole in the door they had just come through. They raced down the alleyway.

"Wait!" Seven-Rings said. "Where are you going?"

"Away from here!" a rat answered.

"But where?" she persisted. As if in answer, the roaring grew louder. Seven-Rings looked up to see the yellow monster's head appear around the back corner of the church. Its great jaws opened, and it bit into the building.

"Who cares? Go!" said a large brown rat as he placed his paws on Seven-Rings's back and pushed. She needed no more urging. Together, the animals raced away as the side of the church collapsed into the alley behind them.

Chapter 2

Seven-Rings and Arnica ran with the rats as fast and as far as they could. Seven had made only brief forays outside of the church with her mother; Arni had been outside only once. The sky, the smells, and their strange companions frightened them, but the yellow monster frightened them more. And Seven realized that the rats knew the best escape route.

After several minutes, the animals paused in the shade of a dumpster behind a fried-chicken restaurant. Although they could no longer see the monster, they could hear it. Its roar was accompanied by the crash and shatter of the old church falling beneath its assault.

Seven and Arni sat up on their haunches as they caught their breath. Arni said, "Mama? Typhoo?"

Summoning all her confidence, Seven replied, "Don't

worry, Arni. I'm sure they'll catch up." After she spoke, one last horrific crash told her that their home was gone. To distract Arnica, she said, "Oh, look! What a pretty acorn!" She scuffed at it with her hind paw.

"Acorn!" said Arni. She released her older sister's paws and picked up the acorn. "It has a pop," she said, referring to the acorn's cap.

"Good! Those are the best kind," Seven said. All the while, she watched the rats. They were speaking quietly among themselves, and every so often a small group broke off and disappeared. Finally, there were only a dozen rats left. They began to drift away.

"That's it, then," said the big brown rat who had pushed Seven-Rings along. "Good luck to you." He turned to follow the others.

"Wait!" said Seven-Rings. "Where are you going?"

The rat looked at her quizzically. "We're off to find a new place to live, of course. Thought you'd be doing the same right about now."

Seven-Rings hesitated, not wanting to show weakness in front of a stranger. She glanced at Arnica, who was turning the acorn over in her paws. "It's just that . . ."

"Oh, I see," said the rat, in a sympathetic voice that startled her. "You're both a bit on the young side, aren't you? Well," he paused, considering, "it wouldn't do for me to be seen with the likes of you. But I can't in good conscience leave you here, either." He paused to think. "I know where another raccoon lives. I'll take you to him. You'll be with your own kind. That's the best I can do." He called to the other rats, "I'm going to take these two to Greyson. I'll meet you at the new site." The other rats stopped and narrowed their eyes for a moment as they studied Seven-Rings and Arnica. Then they nodded and continued on their way.

"This way," the rat said. Without waiting to see if they were following, he ran under the gate next to the dumpster.

Seven-Rings tugged gently on her sister's foreleg. Arnica put the acorn into her cheek and dropped to all fours. Then she and her sister squeezed under the gate.

Before them lay a parking lot, fading yellow stripes painted on the cracked black asphalt. The rat was standing in the shadow of the scrubby trees that grew just across the lot. "Come on! Get a move on!" he called.

The rat led them around the building, down a broad alleyway that was lined with broken-down cars and trucks, and under a chain-link fence. Eager to complete his errand, the rat moved fast, ducking and dodging around empty boxes and rusting metal objects. The sour, greasy smell turned Seven-Rings's stomach. She glanced back and felt heartened by the sight of Arnica running behind her, her left cheek puffed out by the acorn.

They traveled until the sun reached its peak, when the rat stopped outside of a brick building. The rat sat up on his haunches and said, "This is Greyson's place."

Seven-Rings sat up and studied the wall before her. "How do we get in?"

The rat shrugged. "Don't know. Good luck." With that, he turned away. In a moment, it was as though he had never existed.

Arnica took the acorn out of her mouth and began to play with it. The abandoned lot was quiet. The presence of tall weeds and the absence of car smells told Seven that there was little danger of them being seen, because humans clearly never came here anymore.

Leaving Arnica in the shade of milkweed plants, Seven-Rings scampered around the outside of the building. Metal grates, darkened with age, covered the first-story windows. Stringy vines clung to the cracked brick walls. On the east wall, she found an old wooden door, but when she pushed on it, it did not budge. On the north wall, she found a rusty ladder that led to an open third-floor window. She jumped to the lowest rung, and the ladder swayed under her slight weight. Seven climbed as quickly as she dared. After a few moments, she perched on the window ledge.

Seven sniffed the ledge and window frame. A musky smell, the scent of a full-grown male raccoon, was quite strong and recent. Whether he had been on his way in or out, she couldn't be sure. She peered inside. A thick layer of dust covered much of the floor, except for the paths that the resident raccoon traveled regularly. Those were patterned with footprints and dusted by sweeps of a bushy tail. More metal things littered the floor, left behind because they were of no use to humans anymore. An old wire ran down the wall near the window. Seven-Rings reached for it, but it was too far away. She stretched, overbalanced, and plunged off the windowsill.

With a scrabble of claws, she managed to catch the end of the wire with her left paw. She swung and smacked hard into the wall. She lost her hold and fell the last few feet to the floor.

The fall made her vision blurry. She shook her head to clear it and moved each limb. Nothing was broken.

Seven-Rings got to her paws, her feet crunching on dry leaves that had blown in through the window. She shivered.

As she turned to go back outside, a furry shape slammed into her and knocked her off her paws. She skidded across the floor. The shape lunged again, and she felt jaws close on the back of her neck.

She mewled in pain and fear. "Don't hurt me!"

After a moment, the jaws released their grip, but large paws still pinned her to the floor. Breath whistled in her ear.

"What do you want?" a voice growled.

"I'm looking for Greyson," she said. "The rat from the church said he could help me—and my sister."

"The church?" The voice sounded puzzled. "That's a

long way away. Are you from the church?"

"Yes. It's gone now. A monster . . ." She choked up as she thought of Mama and Typhoo.

The pressure on her back let up. Cautiously, she turned her head and saw a raccoon at least four times her size, twice as big as her mother. His brown pelt was flecked with gray. One eye glittered in his black mask; in the place of the other one was an ugly scar. His forepaws were gnarled like the branches of an old tree, but the claws were long and sharp. Seven-Rings trembled and looked away.

"Don't worry," he said in a voice that was as rusty as the machines. "You've nothing to fear from me. Get up."

Seven did as he said, trying to hide the fact that she was shaking.

"My name is Greyson."

"I'm Seven-Rings Moon," Seven replied. "My sister Arnica is outside."

"You lived in the church," Greyson mused. "Are you a child of Runner Moon?"

"Yes, sir. Runner Moon is my mother."

"And your sister is outside?" When Seven nodded, Greyson replied, "I'll go get her." Without another word, he ran to the window and leaped. He vanished down the ladder.

Seven-Rings scrambled madly upward. She reached the sill in time to see Greyson land silently behind Arnica, who was right where Seven-Rings had left her, holding her acorn. He seized her by the scruff of the neck, and she squealed in fright as they started back up the rusty ladder.

"It's OK, Arni!" Seven-Rings called as loudly as she could. "He's a friend!" Despite his size, Greyson moved like lightning. Seven-Rings hastily jumped out of his way, and he barreled through the window. They landed with a soft thump. Eyes screwed shut, Arni mewled in fear, although Greyson released her gently.

Seven-Rings put her forelegs around her terrified sibling and said, "Shh, shh, it's all right." She rocked her sister until she quieted down. "See, Arni? It's all right. We're together."

The tiny raccoon pressed her face into her big sister's chest.

Greyson sat on his haunches and watched the sisters with interest. "She is very small," Greyson said, matter-of-factly.

"She was born last," Seven explained. "Mama said that it took a long time for her eyes and ears to open. And she had a hard time staying warm. But she'll be all right."

"Life will be difficult for her."

"I will take care of her," Seven said. A wave of confidence swept over her as she held her little sister.

The giant raccoon looked pleased by the answer. "You are truly like your mother."

Seven said, "Do you know her?"

Greyson nodded. "I do. She is my daughter."

"That means you're—," she began.

He nodded his heavy head. "I am your grandfather." The way he looked at her made her wonder, and then he said, "I wish I'd come to see you. But that's our way, from the time of First Raccoon. Males live alone, and females live with the kits."

"The church—it's gone," blurted Seven. "Mama told me to run, so Arnica and I did."

"And a rat brought you here," Greyson said.

"Yes, sir. He lived in the basement. He ran out when we did. Everyone left—the bats, the rats. Us."

Seven's worry about Mama and Typhoo threatened to

spill out, but instead, she hugged Arni more tightly. Now over her scare, Arni turned her head to study Greyson. She held out her paw and offered him the acorn.

"Thank you, small one. Perhaps we can play later. Right now, I think we should eat. I know just the thing. While I am out, rest and explore. There are many exits if you need them, but you should be safe here." He launched himself to the windowsill and left.

Arnica leaned back and looked in Seven's eyes. "He's really big!"

Seven chirped with amusement. "He is, isn't he? He's family, though. We don't have anything to be afraid of."

At least for now, she thought.

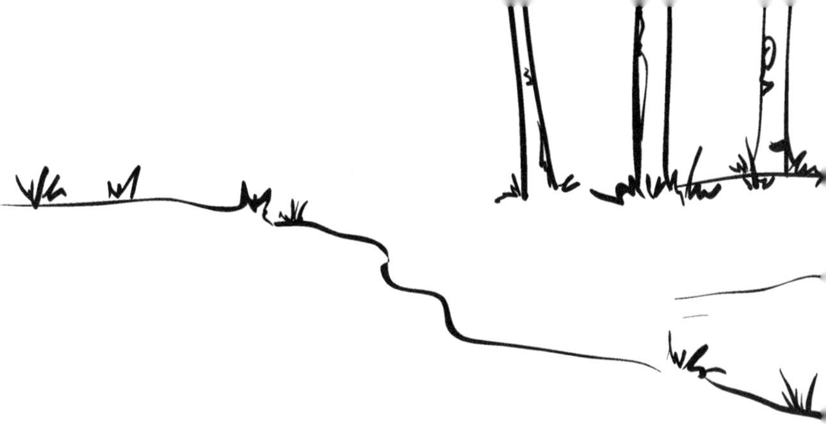

Chapter 3

When the sun had moved a tail's length across the floor, Greyson returned. He carried a white paper bag in his teeth. The scent of fried chicken wafted from the bag, and Seven's and Arni's mouths began to water.

As she munched on a biscuit, Seven thought of how odd it was to not wrestle with Typhoo for her fair share. Suddenly the biscuit seemed dry and flavorless, and she put it down.

Greyson watched her with his good eye. "What's wrong?" He tore a french fry in half and swallowed it down.

Seven shook her head, unwilling to speak in front of Arnica.

"I can guess," the male raccoon said. "Life is dangerous, Seven. The world makes no promises to anyone. No promises that we will be happy, or even safe." She stared at him. "Your mother never spoke so bluntly, did she?" he said, and then chuckled. "Runner has always been an optimist. That's one thing about the Moon family—all optimists, every last one. I don't understand what your grandmother saw in me. Maybe opposites attract."

He paused, and Seven saw a glimmer of fond remembrance in his eye. Then he seemed to realize she was watching him, and said abruptly, "You will have to be smart and cunning. Brave, too, especially given the name you carry."

Seven said to Greyson, "What do you mean?"

"Surely, Runner must have told you," Greyson said.

Seven shook her head.

Greyson's scarred face softened. "There is a legend. It says that in a month in which there is a copper-colored moon, a raccoon with seven black rings on its tail will be born."

Seven looked at him in wonder. "Mama said the moon was copper the night we were born."

Greyson nodded wisely. "It is said that this raccoon will have a rare gift. Only very few creatures can find the Notch, and only this raccoon can save it."

"The Notch? What's that?"

"The Notch is the heart of the forest, where sap still runs in trees older than any animal can remember. It is a safe place for the creatures of the woods and the birds of the air. The Notch is a place where people cannot go. The sides are too steep for humans and their machines to climb down. Only the four-legged and the feathered can navigate the slopes that lead into the Notch.

"I've never seen it, myself," Greyson continued. "I'm a city raccoon, just as you are. We live with people. But there was a time when all raccoons lived in places with trees as tall as buildings, and where the ground was soil and soft moss. Didn't your mother tell you?"

Seven shook her head.

"The story of the Notch is the story of all raccoons, and, indeed, of all animals." Greyson said. He sat up on his haunches and his one good eye sparkled as he spoke. "When the world was young, it was all flat and smooth, as flat as this floor. One morning, after it had rained all night, First Raccoon and all the other First Animals emerged from their sleeping places to find that the land was covered with water. They struggled and splashed. First Deer could not eat, because all the plants were under water. First Rabbit's warren had flooded, and she and her babies shivered because they were soaking wet. Smaller animals were in danger of drowning altogether.

"So First Raccoon got to work. She began to dig a long, deep hole. When the other First Animals saw what she was doing, they joined in. Together, the First Animals dug a huge trench, and the water rushed into it. That became the first river. They piled the dirt from the trench up high and formed the first mountain. The water drained away, and the ground was dry again.

"The First Animals were so happy and relieved! They decided to reward First Raccoon for her cleverness and hard work. They climbed up First Mountain and dug a hollow valley into the mountainside. They lined it with trees, just as First Raccoon liked, and filled the bottom of the valley with ponds and berry bushes. First Wolf explained that it was called the Notch, and it was a place for First Raccoon and all who need a safe haven."

Seven-Rings shook her head. "I can't imagine such a place," she said.

"It's your destiny," Greyson responded. "You're not only meant to go there, Seven. You're also meant to save it, to stop those who would destroy it."

"Me?" she squeaked. "What can I do? I'm only a little raccoon."

"Even the greatest things start small. The story says that only you can save this treasured place."

"But I don't want to go to the Notch."

Greyson shrugged. "Wanting means nothing. You've already started the journey."

"No, no, there's no journey," Seven said. "We just . . . we had to run, and then the rat told me he knew where there was another raccoon, and . . ." Her voice trailed off.

Greyson picked up another french fry and bit into it. "You can't change destiny, Seven-Rings Moon," he said. "You must find the Notch, Seven, and protect it from whatever threat that it is under."

"What threat?"

Greyson shook his head. "I do not know—I am an old city raccoon. As you travel, listen; you'll find out what needs to be done. You must go there to be safe. And not just for yourself, but for Arnica, too, and for all the other creatures, furred and feathered, who seek shelter there."

"You come, too, Greyson!" Arni said.

"Oh, yes, please!" Seven said. "You have to!"

Greyson shook his head. "I'm too old."

"No, you're not," Seven said. "You have to come with us. We're family."

"The trip will be long and difficult."

Seven rubbed her head against Greyson's massive shoulder. "Mama always says that as long as you are not alone, nothing is difficult."

The old male raccoon looked from one to the other of his grandkits, as though trying to think of another reason but finding none. "You're just like your grandmother, Seven-Rings Moon," he said. "You don't take no for an answer! We'll leave in the morning."

Arnica yawned hugely and curled up against Seven. "Story," she said softly.

At Greyson's puzzled look, Seven explained, "Mama tells us stories when she wants us to sleep."

"I can do that," Greyson said. He cleared his throat and began.

"One day, First Raccoon was sitting by a stream, waiting for dinner to swim near. It was her favorite fishing spot. But on this day, she was not alone. A new creature—with no fur and no tail—was splashing around, trying desperately to catch a fish. First Raccoon watched for a moment. 'You'll scare all the fish away,' she said.

"The tailless creature stopped its splashing. 'They are so fast!' it said.

"First Raccoon took pity on the tailless thing. 'You need to sit quietly and wait,' she explained. So the tailless thing came out of the water and sat next to her. They waited quietly together, and eventually the fish returned.

" 'Now, I'll show you how,' said First Raccoon. She leaned out over the water, balancing herself with her tail, and swiftly caught a fish. But when the tailless creature tried, it fell smack into the water. It couldn't balance. First Raccoon's way of catching fish wasn't going to work. She wanted to help the poor hungry tailless one, so she gave it some fish and suggested they meet at the same spot the next day. As she took the rest of the catch to her kits, she saw a spider dangling from its web. That gave her an idea.

"She worked long into the night on her gift for the tailless creature. It was a stick with a thin but strong thread of grass fibers tied to one end. At the end of the thread was a down feather that looked for all the world like a white spider. As soon as First Raccoon held the pole out over the water, a fish leaped up to catch the down feather. She jerked the pole, and the fish flew onto the bank.

"The tailless thing tried the device and soon got the hang of it. It gave the first fishes it caught to First Raccoon as a thank-you gift. As she took the food to her family, First Raccoon could hear the tailless one laughing with delight as it caught fish after fish."

By the time the story was finished, Arni had dozed off on top of Seven, as she often did. Greyson stood up and shook himself. "I'd better find us something to eat before we go," he said. "There's no telling where our next meal will come from once we leave here."

Worn out by the day's events, Seven closed her eyes. She woke frequently, and each time she noted the progress of the moonlight across the floor. The night was nearly over, and there was no sign of Greyson.

She dozed again, then suddenly woke to a crash. Greyson and a large black-and-brown dog cannoned into the large room. Greyson's erect fur made him look nearly as big as his tormentor. Teeth bared, he lashed out at the dog with his claws. "Get out of my house, you flea-bitten bag of filth!" Greyson hissed.

"Filth! You are the filth, mad one!" the dog snarled back. "I'll rip you to shreds!"

Arnica was awake, her eyes huge with fear as she watched the fight. Quietly, Seven began urging her toward the drain in the floor. Together they tugged on the cover, willing it to come loose.

The dog spun toward the sound. He had slobbering jaws, a blocklike skull, and trunklike legs that ended in massive paws. His lips curled back as he looked at the sisters, revealing sharp yellow teeth.

Quickly, Greyson said, "I told you, fool, I did not give your mate and pups the Madness! If I had, I would be dead already!"

"Gone! Because of you!" the dog howled, and the pain in his voice felt like a physical blow to Seven.

"Dog! Listen to me! You have no cause to seek revenge! We are innocent!" Greyson kept himself between the furious dog and Seven and Arnica.

"No! Your kind are never innocent!"

Seven shoved Arnica into the drain and jumped in after her just as the dog lunged for Greyson.

The drain led straight down, and the two raccoons fell for what seemed to be forever. The snarling of the big raccoon and the angry dog faded as they fell, and vanished entirely as they landed with a splash.

Sputtering, Seven-Rings burst to the surface into the darkness. Her whiskers told her she was inside a tube. Water tugged at her fur and whirled her around. Her claws scraped against the curved walls as the pipe spilled out into another, larger pipe. "Arnica!" she called through sodden whiskers. There was no answer. "Arni!"

Panic rose in Seven's throat, but she swallowed hard and kicked forward with all her strength. At last, her forepaw touched familiar fur. She gathered her sister to her and strained her eyes to see where the water was carrying them.

Chapter 4

Splat! Seven and Arnica tumbled out of the drain and on to an expanse of puddly mud. Their abrupt arrival sent half a dozen white herring gulls squawking into the air. A larger gull with a black back and wings stepped back a pace and regarded them coolly with her yellow eyes. Seven-Rings positioned herself between her sister and the black-backed gull and tried to look relaxed while Arni began to dry herself.

The bird watched them for a moment. Then she said, "A rough landing, that."

Seven-Rings nodded. Although she had never met a black-backed gull before, she sensed the big bird's solemnity, so unlike that of her herring-gull relatives who were squawking and fighting on a sandbar in the middle of the river. The gull preened her feathers. "But any landing where you don't break a wing is a good one, I suppose."

"I suppose so," Seven answered politely.

The gull cocked her head and looked from Seven to Arni and back. "You don't belong in a pipe, and you don't belong to the sea," the gull said matter-of-factly.

"No, you're right," Seven said. "We were with our grandfather in a building. Then there was a dog. We just wanted to hide."

"We don't have many fur-faces around here," said the gull. "Mostly gulls, some egrets, an arrogant heron or two. But no fur-faces." At the look on Seven's face, the bird said hastily, "No offense is meant. Fur-face is not a bad word."

"It doesn't sound exactly complimentary," Seven said.

"I shall be more careful. I have spoken to your kind only once before, on a beach far to the south, where the turtles lay their eggs, and the robbers come and steal them."

"Robbers?"

"Like you. With masks and ringed tails."

Seven realized that the gull was speaking of other raccoons. "Is it far?" she asked, thinking that perhaps she and Arni could find them.

"Not far to fly, but for legs like yours, too far . . . too far, too far." The gull paused, then said, "Because I have talked to creatures like you before, I talk to you now. I know I am too big for you to hurt. But you are not too big for me to hurt."

Seven-Rings held up her paws, palms up, beseechingly.

"Please, we are just young, and we've lost our home." She told the gull the story of the yellow monster. The gull listened with keen interest, and when Seven finished, she said, "I have seen things like that. Ma-sheens. They have humans in them."

"But why would the humans destroy our home?"

The gull said, "The human in the ma-sheen probably didn't even know you were there. There is much they miss. They are different from the rest of us."

An idea struck Seven. "You said you've talked to other raccoons like us. Did they ever talk about a place without people?"

The gull closed her eyes in thought. After a moment, she said, "I heard once. Three robbers—sloppy with eggs, silly with food—they sang and made much noise. The song was about a place called the Notch."

"The Notch! That's where we want to go. Can you tell me anything else?"

"It is north, where it gets cold, though not so far that it is icy all the time. I don't know how far—the song didn't say."

Seven exclaimed, "Thank you! We will find it." Excited, she turned to Arnica. Her sister was sound asleep, exhausted.

The gull clacked her bill softly, and the sound was kind. "Sleep first, it looks like. Then follow the river against the flow. That will be a start. Rest now, I will watch over you. No harm will come. I promise."

When Seven and Arnica woke, they discovered that the great gull had gathered a pile of clams and mussels in a pool of water. After watching them struggle with the unfamiliar food, she showed them how to crack the shells on rocks. The gull watched them eat, and, then, wishing them fair winds, she spread her wide wings and flew away.

Once she became no more than a dot in the distance, Seven and Arnica began walking north, against the flow of the river. They walked in the shallows, enjoying the water and mud on their paws, and splashing at each other. Arnica lunged for Seven-Rings, and they fell head over tail into the river itself.

They wrestled for a few moments, then Arnica shrieked. Seven jumped backwards. Arnica twisted around, and a massive head rose out of the water. A monstrous fish held Arni by the tail.

Without thinking, Seven leaped onto the fish's head, biting hard at the base of its neck. The fish thrashed as it tried to dislodge its attacker. Jaws locked, Seven twisted around and scratched at the fish's eyes. She felt a soft pop, and the fish shuddered and made a thunderous rumble deep inside its body. It flung itself back toward the middle of the river. Seven flew off and landed hard on the bank. She

jumped up, hissing with anger and fear, but the monster fish was gone.

"Arni! Are you all right?"

"Tail . . . hurts!" Seven-Rings's stomach turned. Most of her little sister's tail was gone. Blood spurted out with each of Arnica's heartbeats. Arnica was breathing hard. Her eyes closed. She collapsed to the bank.

"Arni!" Seven exclaimed.

A mouse appeared suddenly and ordered, "Put your paws on it! Hard!"

Seven did as the mouse said, while he scratched at the bank and swiftly rolled up a small ball of mud. "Now move," he commanded. Seven pulled her paw away, and the mouse placed a mud ball firmly on the wound. The mud sealed the wound. "She's coming around."

As Arni groaned, Seven asked, "What was that creature?"

"It was a pike," the mouse answered, scanning the water for any sign of the monster. "He's been in this stretch of river forever. Eats anything he can catch." He scampered to a nearby tree, from which he tore off a strip of bark. He brought it to Arni. "Here, chew on this. It'll help the hurt." As she took the bark, the mouse said, "Not from around here, are you?"

"Is it that obvious?" Seven asked.

Arni chewed the bark and the pain in her tail eased. As she chewed, the mouse disappeared briefly and returned with a long, narrow leaf and a length of stringy grass. Deftly, he placed the leaf over Arnica's wound and wrapped it snugly with the grass.

"Thank you," Arni said. Seven nodded.

The tiny creature said only, "This is a dangerous place. Keep your wits about you." Then he was gone, the only evidence of his existence the bandage on Arni's tail.

Wounded and wary, the sisters continued on, keeping away from the water.

Chapter 5

The sisters traveled as quickly as they could, walking night and day. The incident with the pike had sobered them. They slept, curled up together, between tree roots and beneath low bushes.

The river flowed through human places, gathering all manner of trash as it did so. Breakfast consisted of whatever could be found: slugs, insects, seeds, cold french fries, or a half-eaten burger. Arnica proved to be very good at finding earthworms. No matter how hard Seven-Rings listened, she could never hear them gliding along in their subterranean tunnels. Her sister would push her gently aside, and then begin to dig and, without fail, soon hold up her prize.

One evening, as they lay curled together under the broad leaves of a bush, watching the rain fall, Arni said, "This is a good night for a story."

Seven didn't say anything, but remembered many rainy nights in the old church when Runner would gather the three of them on the couch in the old parlor and tell them tales of First Raccoon. They loved the stories, even though Typhoo usually fell asleep halfway through. Or maybe that was part of the reason they loved stories, because their boisterous brother would finally quiet down. Seven tried not to focus on how much she missed Typhoo, Runner—and Greyson, for that matter—as she searched her memory for a good story.

"OK," said Seven. "In the early days of the world, all the First Animals were awake during the day and slept all night—except for one. First Owl slept all day and was awake at night, so she could protect the world of the night.

"Every morning, First Raccoon woke up, stretched, and went to her favorite spot for crayfish. Then she worked with the other First Animals to get the world in order. But on this day, someone had already eaten all the crayfish within reach, and all the ones that remained were hiding under rocks on the bottom. First Raccoon studied the soft ground and recognized the footprints of First Possum.

"When First Raccoon found First Possum, she asked, 'Why did you get up so early? All of us sleep until dawn, except for First Owl. Why have you changed the order of things?'

"First Possum did not answer.

"First Raccoon stalked away, angry that First Possum had messed up her crayfish hole. When she saw her friend, First Crow, she told him all about what had happened.

"First Crow said, 'You are going to have to get up earlier if you don't want to go hungry.'

"So that evening, First Raccoon asked First Owl to wake her early. And she did, waking First Raccoon when the moon was high up in the sky. First Raccoon went to the crayfish pool and ate her fill. When First Possum came to the pool, First Raccoon was just finishing her last crayfish.

He glared at First Raccoon with his beady black eyes and stomped away.

"And so it began. The next day, First Possum beat First Raccoon to the pool, and the day after that, First Raccoon won. Back and forth they went, sometimes sleeping all day and staying awake all night, and sometimes sleeping all night and staying awake all day. Day and night no longer meant anything to them. They developed a habit of eating when they were hungry and sleeping when they were tired. And we do that still, because we never want other creatures, especially possums, to get the better of us."

Seven knew by Arni's breathing that she had fallen asleep before the story was half finished, but she kept telling the story until the end. After a moment of silence, she heard a rustle of wings, and a crow peeked down at her through the leaves.

"You are a wonderful storyteller," said the crow.

Pleased at the compliment, Seven said, "Thank you. I come from a long line of storytellers."

"I can see that. Are you hungry?"

"A little."

The crow vanished. Seven waited, curious to see what would happen next. The crow returned, holding a plastic package containing a single hot dog.

"I hope you don't mind them raw," the crow said. "I prefer them after the humans have heated them up, but this was the best I could do. Although they were busy eating, it's risky to get too close to them. They often dislike my kind." The crow bobbed her head. "Please, eat. It's our custom to show our appreciation for a good story with a gift. I thought that food would be more practical than a button or a stone."

Thanking the crow, Seven bit into the hot dog. She had never had one before. "This is delicious!" she said.

"One of my favorite things," the crow said. She looked pleased that Seven liked the gift.

"Would you like some?" Seven offered, remembering her manners.

The crow took a tiny bite, just to be sociable. Seven ate about half of the hot dog, then slipped the rest into the package, to give Arni when she woke up.

"So you are looking for a new territory?" asked the crow.

Seven shook her head.

The crow looked at her intently, and Seven felt that the bird was doing some serious thinking. "Aha!" the crow said at last. "You're going to the Notch."

"How do you know?"

The crow shook her wings. "You have seven rings on your tail. Also, you seem to have been born five months ago, during the time of the copper moon. All wild things know the story of the Notch, and how it will be saved by a very special raccoon—one with seven rings who was born during the copper moon." The crow paused and then explained, "We crows know the story of how the Notch came to be, and how First Crow planted all the trees there." They were silent for a moment, and then the crow added, "It is a long way."

Seven nodded. "That's what the gull said."

The crow cocked an eye toward the sleeping Arni. "She is a smallish nestling," the crow said, trying to sound as kind as she could.

"She was the smallest of our litter," Seven said. "Typhoo, our brother, was going to be bigger than the two of us combined."

"Was?"

"I don't know whether Typhoo is still alive. Or my mother." Seven's voice cracked.

The crow responded, "Knowing and not knowing are equally hard, but different. My father was flying with me, teaching me all his tricks. He landed in the middle of the road. A cry from a hawk distracted him, and he was hit by a car."

"I'm sorry," Seven said sincerely.

The crow ruffled her feathers, as if to throw off the sadness. "It was a long time ago. Now I have no one to care for. I am looking for a new territory. Would you like some company?"

Seven looked at the crow's broad, fierce bill and sharp

talons, and then at her kind eyes. It would be good to have a friend, she thought.

"I am Brangwy," the crow said, dipping her head.

"I'm Seven-Rings, and this is Arnica."

"I will watch the little one. You go find some more food. A hot dog is not enough for a long trip."

Seven-Rings trundled off into the undergrowth. It was nice to move on her own, without having to keep one eye on Arnica, although she felt guilty for thinking it. The hot dog had whet her appetite, and when she found a stash of wild mushrooms, the meal was complete. She carried a few back to where Arni and Brangwy were getting acquainted.

"Seven! This is a nice bird," Arni exclaimed when she saw her sister emerge from the tall grasses. "She gave me a treat."

"And I have more treats for you," Seven said, handing over the mushrooms. Arni stuffed the mushrooms into her mouth, coughing a little because there were more than she had bargained for. Brangwy led them to a nearby stream for a deep drink, and then the sisters and their new friend were on the road again.

Chapter 6

The crow proved to be an excellent companion, always alert and curious, and full of news about the world. As she listened to Brangwy's tales, Seven realized how little she knew, especially when Brangwy described things she had never heard of, such as swimming pools ("They look like ponds, but the water tastes awful"); trains ("long, loud metal snakes"); and airplanes ("They look like birds that are flying very high, but up close they are huge!"). When Seven described the yellow monster, Brangwy nodded sagely. "I've seen those machines," she said. "They make quick work of buildings."

One morning, not long after Arnica's tail had formed a scab, they came to the banks of a broad body of water. They looked west and east, and could not see the end of the water. The water stretched farther north than they could see, too.

As Brangwy flew upward to see if the water ended, Seven lapped at it. "I think it's a big river."

"Do we swim?" Arnica asked. She shuddered at the thought.

Brangwy landed next to Arni with a flutter of wings. "It's very wide," she said. "I don't think you can swim."

Seven glanced at Arni, who was trying to hide her discomfort at the idea of swimming in any body of water. "We'll just go around, then," she said. She raised her nose and sniffed the air. There was a strange smell, like the smell of the church's old chimney, only sharper. She followed her nose, and Arni followed her. Brangwy fluttered from tree to tree above them.

After they climbed over a small rise in the forest floor, the raccoons saw a burned cabin. Only the west wall of the cabin was still standing; the rest of the walls had fallen outward, and the roof was completely gone. Black ash clung to the wooden beams and posts like scales on a lizard. Curiously shaped lumps stood here and there. The smell of wet ash hung in the air, the ghost of the flames.

Closer to the waterline, a picnic table stood unscathed, far enough from the cabin that the fire had not reached it. A cooler sat on the ground next to the table, as if waiting for the humans to return. Seven pushed the plastic lid off the cooler to see if there was anything inside. The lid hit the ground and slid across the small rocks that covered the beach.

Seven leaped on the lid. "Whee!" she cried.

Brangwy landed on the picnic table and watched Seven slide with interest. Arni crept across the stones, uncertain about this peculiar behavior on her sister's part.

"Look!" Seven-Rings clambered off the lid and pushed it toward Arni. "It can slide, see?" She ran a little ways off, turned, and jumped on the lid. It skidded all the way down the beach and into the shallow water. The lid floated.

"I bet you can get across if you ride on this," Brangwy said.

Arnica crept cautiously over to the lid and sniffed it. "It's OK. Get on," Seven urged. Arnica scrambled aboard the makeshift craft, and, after giving the lid a mighty push, Seven jumped on behind her.

The water's movement pushed the lid gently back to shore. It bumped against the pebbles.

"You have to get it out farther," said the crow helpfully.

Without thinking, Seven jumped into the water and began to push.

Arni's fur puffed up. "Fish! Fish!" she cried. "Get out! Big fish will get you!"

Seven looked around wildly, but she saw only a couple of minnows. As fast as she could, she pushed the lid into deeper water. Soon her paws were no longer touching the bottom. "Arni! Help me!" she said.

But her sister did not move.

Gripping hard, Seven tried to drag herself aboard. "Arni! Give me your paw!" Then she saw a hole in the surface of the lid; she stretched her right foreleg as far as she could and snagged it with one claw. She pulled herself

onto the raft. After catching her breath, she crawled over and shook Arnica. "Arni! Arni, wake up!"

Arni's eyes were open. In them Seven-Rings saw only terror. She wrapped her forelegs around her sister and held her. As the crow circled above, they drifted out toward the center of the lake.

Seven-Rings was not nearly as afraid as Arnica was, although she did hope that the lake contained no pikes. While Arni sat in the center of the lid, careful to keep far from the water, Seven lay flat on her stomach and peered down into the lake, marveling at the forms of fish and rocks that she could see below. She did not notice the gray clouds coming together in the east, or the sudden increase in the wind. When Brangwy cried, "Caw-caw-caw!" Seven looked up in surprise.

"Storm!" cried the crow. "Rain and wind, on the way! I will be back!" She tipped her wings and zoomed away.

"We need to go in, then," Arnica said. "Mama said go in if it rains."

Seven looked around helplessly. There was no *in* to go to, no shelter here on the water.

"I think we're going to have to hold on tight, Arni," she said. With teeth and claws, she ripped at the plastic and cut enough paw holds for them both. Spitting out bits of plastic, she said, "Lie down, Arni, and hold on." She guided her sister's hind paws to two holes, saying, "This is like the game we used to play on the sofa, where we'd dig in and see who could hang on the longest."

Arnica said, "I was good at that."

"And I'll bet you'll be good at this game, too," Seven said. A fat raindrop hit her square between the ears. The storm had arrived.

Fat raindrops pelted the two raccoons. Hailstones hissed into the water nearby and bounced off their makeshift raft and their bodies. Lightning dazzled their eyes, and thunder made them flatten their ears. The lake water splashed over them until they were soaked and shivering. The raft bucked and twisted, and without the grips Seven had gnawed, they would have been swept into the water and drowned. The waves and the wind turned the little craft so much that it was impossible to tell which way was north. Would they find themselves back at the cabin? Would they find themselves somewhere else? Would they make it anywhere?

Lightning split the sky and Seven squeezed her eyes even tighter.

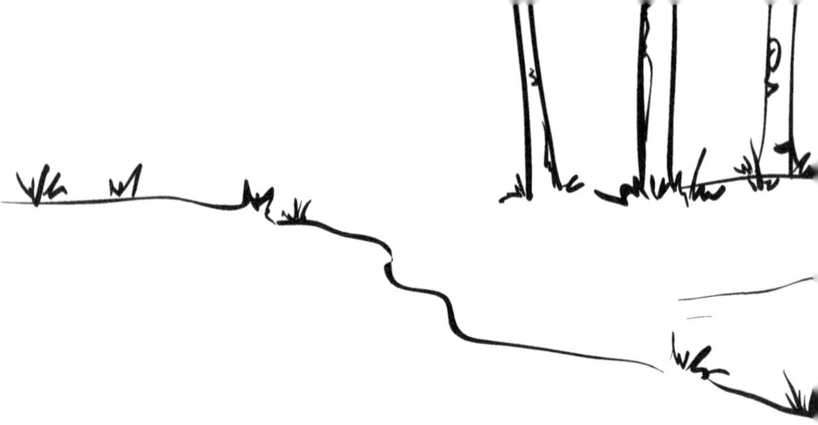

CHAPTER 7

Suddenly their raft shuddered, making Seven's heart skip. She heard the scrape of plastic over pebbles, and she realized they had come to shore. She opened her eyes. Arni was still next to her, flattened and soaked, but still there, and still alive.

"Arni! Let's go! Quick, before we get swept out again." Hearing the urgency in Seven's voice, Arni clambered to her paws and, together, they bounded to the shelter of a nearby highbush blueberry shrub.

They winced at the lightning and shivered at the rolling thunder. They closed their eyes when the wind blew. Gradually, the clouds cleared. The rain stopped, and the wind died down. The air was fresh and bright, and they stepped out from under the blueberry's sheltering branches into a forest that had been scrubbed clean, as if there had never been a storm at all. Their raft was gone, and there was no sign of Brangwy.

"Where's the nice bird?" Arni asked.

Seven shook her head. "I don't know, Arni." She felt saddened by the loss of their companion.

Arnica gave a smart nod. "She'll be back. Don't worry."

Wishing she could feel as confident as her sister did, Seven-Rings took a deep sniff. She no longer smelled the burned cabin, but she did smell something else, and soon she saw it: a fat little animal, almost as broad as it was long, walking with a rolling gait, its toes pointing in. Its fur was shiny and black, except for the white stripe on its nose and along its back. The older, female skunk squinted as she walked, stopping to sniff and scratch at the ground experimentally, and then she sneezed. "Is that you, Fungo?" she asked.

"Er, no, it's us," Seven answered. "Seven-Rings and Arnica Moon."

"Moon, is it? That's a raccoon surname, if I'm not mistaken. That must make you raccoons." The skunk squinted hard at them and must have seen their masks, for she said, "Yep, you're raccoons. Good, b'cause I've got no patience with otters. Silly creatures."

Mildly confused at this non-sequitur, Seven-Rings and Arnica sat silent as the skunk continued chatting. "We've been missing a good strong raccoon presence here since the

Madness swept through five years ago. You haven't got the Madness, have you? No, of course you don't, because those with the Madness aren't nice and polite like you two. There are two of you, aren't there?"

"Yes, ma'am," answered Seven. The sisters stepped apart so the skunk could see them clearly.

"How'd you come to be here?" the skunk asked.

"We came across the big water," Seven said.

"The big water? Oh, you mean the lake, of course. Never seen a lake before, have you? No, of course you haven't, because you'd be calling it a lake and not a big water if you had. And how did you come across the lake?"

"We floated!" Arnica piped up.

"Floated? Floated?" The skunk stamped her feet. "What do you take me for, an otter? That lake's too wide for the likes of you—or anyone, for that matter—to float over. Besides, that storm would have drowned you."

"But we're telling the truth. We did float. On a human thing we found at a burned house," said Seven-Rings. "It's gone now. The water washed it away."

Muttering skeptically and clearly not convinced the raccoons were telling the truth, the skunk tottered to the water's edge. After sniffing and scratching, she agreed that they could have indeed floated across the lake. Suddenly, the skunk's facial expression changed from skepticism to curiosity. "What is your name again?" she said.

"Seven-Rings Moon."

The curiosity changed to delight. "The Moon has come over the water—by the spray of First Skunk! Well, now, Moon sisters, you just come with me. I've got a dry, safe burrow where you can tell me all about your adventures, and I can tell you what I know. My name is Fig." With that, the skunk turned and waddled quickly toward the trees. Mystified, Seven and Arni looked at each other.

"I guess it's OK," Seven said. And with that, they followed the skunk. Fig's burrow was a large, fine, deep hole between the roots of an oak tree. Arni's eyes lit up. "Acorns!" she shouted, and raced to the tree, where she began tossing the nuts into the air.

Fig looked at her curiously and turned to Seven-Rings. "Is she always like this?"

Seven-Rings shrugged. "She likes acorns." She convinced Arni to leave most of the acorns outside and enter Fig's burrow. Once inside, Arni contented herself with rolling the acorns across the floor, trying to hit one with another.

Fig pointed to Arnica's tail. "Dog?" she asked.

"Fish, actually," Seven-Rings answered. "The mouse we met called it a pike."

Fig shuddered. "Nasty big brutes, those. They're afraid of nothing and no one, not even humans. If fish could have the Madness, they'd all be pikes. You were lucky to survive."

She paused to think. "I heard about a raccoon that attacked a pike. That was you, wasn't it?"

"How did you hear?"

Fig chuckled. "A bird must have seen your adventure. The best way to spread news is to tell a bird. They're terrible gossips, those feathered folk, but they come in handy at times. Squirrels, too, if you can get one of the tree people to slow down long enough to listen to you."

Arnica looked up from where she was rolling the acorns. "The mouse gave me bark. My tail stopped hurting."

Fig nodded. "Willow bark. Good for what ails you. Remember that."

It was Seven's turn to nod. The warmth and coziness of the den were making her sleepy. The skunk's scent was milder here, or perhaps she had just gotten used to it. She was beginning to nod off when she felt Fig's roughened paw pads on her foreleg. "Your sister's asleep. Now we can talk."

Seven and Fig went back outside. The woods had come alive and were now full of chirps and chitters, yips and yaps. Fig ignored all these signs of life and faced Seven. She said, "You've come from across the water, just as we've always said you would."

"We who?" Seven asked.

"The descendants of First Skunk, of course," said Fig. "My mother told me the story, just as her mother told her: In a time of terrible need, the Moon would come across the water and save the woods. First Skunk knew everything that would happen. But I never dreamed I'd be the one alive to see the prediction fulfilled."

"Is this the Notch?" Seven asked, confused.

"No, no. This is the lake woods. The Notch is a whole 'nother place." The skunk's nearsighted eyes sparkled. "And a whole 'nother prediction. Who would have guessed that one raccoon was meant by both?"

Seven's mind reeled. It was hard enough to comprehend that First Raccoon had destined her for something—and now First Skunk as well? She said, "I don't understand. Everything seems fine here."

"Follow me," said Fig. They headed up a hill, away from the water. Unfamiliar birds called to each other in the trees above their heads, and chipmunks sat up on stones to watch their passing, chittering to each other behind cupped paws. In the distance, crows swore loudly, and Seven wondered where Brangwy was.

At the top of the hill, they could see dozens upon dozens of houses. They were all the same shape, but different colors. Some had small concrete ponds behind them—the swimming pools that Brangwy had described, while others had concrete clearings. Gray roads ran between the houses, creating a perfect pattern of parallel lines. It was plain even to Seven with her limited experience that these houses were marching up the hill.

"The people are coming," Fig said. "They want to come all the way to the lake. And they have to come through us to do it. Some of us will be able to adapt, like the squirrels. Most of us won't. The birds, for instance—they'll fly away to try to find new homes." She shook her head sorrowfully. "For most of the creatures here, those houses are a death sentence." She pointed at the base of the hill, where bright orange ribbons fluttered from short wooden sticks driven into the ground. "That is how they mark their territory. Before long, the machines will come. They will tear out the trees to make room for the houses. You have to stop them."

A voice came from above them. "Are you hoping against hope, Fig?"

The skunk sniffed upwards into the tree, just to confirm the identity of the speaker. "You know I never lose hope, Merriweather," she said.

The large barred owl spread his wings and glided silently to the ground in front of them. Seven-Rings was glad Arnica was not with them, for the owl was a terrifying sight. He towered over them. His black eyes did not move; he had to turn his head to look at each of them. "Who's your young friend?"

"This is Seven-Rings Moon. She has come over the water to save us," Fig announced, to Seven's distress.

"Well, I—" she began.

"Fig, you are placing too much faith in an old story," Merriweather said gently. To Seven, he said, "I know of the Moon clan. They are fine beasts—honorable and brave. Far too good for city living, if you ask me."

Fig stamped her forepaws impatiently. "It is not a story.

It came from First Skunk herself. Enough chatter. We must stop the houses. She can do it. Her tail has seven rings."

"Really? Then she is a most unusual raccoon."

"No, I'm just a regular raccoon," Seven thought.

"Will you help us?" Fig asked.

Part of Seven wanted to refuse, but she thought of Fig's warm burrow where her sister was safely asleep. She thought of the chipmunks and the birds, of all the unseen creatures that had flooded the air with sound. They needed someone.

"I don't know if I can," Seven said, "but I'll try." Fig squealed with delight, and Merriweather narrowed his eyes in owlish pleasure.

Seven, Fig, and Merriweather spent the day atop the hill, watching the human workers come and go. Before the sun fell, the humans packed up their gear, got into their trucks, and left the site.

"Will they be back?" Seven asked Fig and Merriweather.

"I don't know," Merriweather admitted.

"I'll wait until dark, and then go down there to get a closer look."

The construction site, although vacant beneath the light of the moon, still vibrated with the activity of the workers and the energy put out by their power tools. Seven smoothed her whiskers to still the vibrations so she could concentrate. She sniffed at the skeleton of the house that was being built.

She wrinkled her nose and turned away from the metal frame to study the floor, a poured concrete pad.

"Amazing how they can make rock, isn't it?" Merriweather said, perched on one of the metal crosspieces above Seven.

"I thought you didn't care for humans."

The owl puffed up his feathers. "They are clever, and I admire cleverness."

Somehow, Seven thought, she had to be more clever than the humans. She sat upright and stared out across the moonlit construction site at other houses in various states of completion. As she looked, she noticed something: the ground was bare and flat around each new building.

She went to the edge of the concrete pad of the house. Her whiskers told her that the pad sat directly on the ground; unlike the old church, there was no basement. No basement to fill with water.

She remembered Runner Moon telling her about the old church, and why it had been abandoned. "The basement was always wet," Runner had said. "Humans don't like water in their living places. It ruins the wood and other things they like to build with."

A cheerful *cr-ak!* startled her and made Merriweather puff up in alarm. "I found you! I found you!" cried Brangwy as she spiraled down out of the sky. "After the storm, I found the thing you floated on, but you were not with it!"

"We got to the shore here, and then the water took the lid back," Seven explained.

The crow landed next to her and ducked her head vigorously up and down in enthusiastic greeting. "I was afraid you were lost." She glanced around quickly and asked, "Where is the little one?"

"She's safe, but I can't say the same for you," rumbled Merriweather, clacking his beak in threat.

"Wait, Merriweather! This is Brangwy. She's my friend." Blinking his eyes slowly and with unmistakable malice, the owl listened to the introduction. His feathers remained fluffed.

Brangwy bowed to the owl, although they were nearly the same size. "Friend Owl, I bring no harm and mean no mischief."

Merriweather seemed satisfied by the crow's formal greeting. He smoothed his feathers with his bill. "Well met, Friend Crow," he replied, just as formally.

Relieved, Seven suggested that they leave the construction area. Merriweather agreed and lifted off from the crossbeam, the downdraft from his massive wings extra-intense as he showed his power. As they watched him fly to the top of the hill, Seven asked, "What was that about?"

Brangwy batted her eyes. "What was what about?"

Seven bowed deeply and imitated the crow's voice, "Friend Owl."

Brangwy moved her shoulders and tipped her head, a crow shrug. "It is custom. We have much to fear from each other. The ancient greeting calls for peace."

"You mean, you can work together?"

"I wouldn't go that far." Her voice was light, but her words were serious.

"Sounds like being a crow is complicated."

Brangwy nodded. "It is. But tell me, what are you doing here?"

The two friends walked along as Seven told the crow about everything that had happened. Brangwy tired of walking and flapped up into the branches of a tree. "I was so afraid that the water had taken you and the little one," the crow confessed.

Seven paused and looked out over the lake. Here was plenty of water. More than enough water. Suddenly she had an idea.

CHAPTER 8

As Seven hoped, the woods were full of burrowers—moles and chipmunks, woodchucks, foxes, mice, rabbits, otters, and even snakes and turtles. All of them were willing to help protect the woods. At the height of the next moon, the burrowers came together on the shore of the lake, and Seven explained what needed to be done.

"Humans need flat, dry ground to build," she explained. "If we can make this ground bad for building, then they will not build here."

"What are you thinking?" asked Fig, who was sitting off to one side with Arni and Merriweather.

"We dig holes, lots of them, but not as deep as we normally would. We need to make sure that the humans will fall into them. They should be just a few inches from the surface."

The burrowers murmured about this. "A shallow tunnel gives no protection," said a fox.

"We don't need protection," said a savvy young mole. "We're diggin' traps."

"In a way, yes," Seven agreed.

"And if we don't have to dig deep, we can dig even faster," said a buck rabbit.

"But won't they just fill in the holes?" asked a sensible snake.

"That's the second part of the plan. We will also dig a tunnel that will bring water from the lake. The ground will be weak and wet."

Merriweather continued Seven's train of thought. "The humans won't want to build anymore."

"We must hurry! And disguise the diggings. We want the humans to think that the problem is the ground, not us," Seven said.

Soon the woods filled with activity. Creatures that would normally be stalking and fleeing each other put aside their differences and used claws and paws for digging as fast as they could. Soon, the ground was crisscrossed with tunnels, invisible from the surface, thanks to a layer of leaves and grass. The animals concentrated on the places that had been marked out with sticks.

Meanwhile, at the shore of the lake, the moles and beavers worked out the details of the tunnel that would

carry the water into the newly dug network. With the help of a dozen rabbits, the moles burrowed through the hill that divided the lake from the place where the humans planned to build. The beavers erected a small, but strong, dam. When all was ready, they would rip out the dam with their teeth.

The animals kept digging even after the sun came up, creating sinkholes where the lake water could collect and form mud pits. "Never met a human yet who likes mud," said Fig.

After days and nights of tremendous effort, the animals completed their work. They gathered again on the lake shore. Once Seven determined that everyone was safely out of the tunnel system, she gave the beavers the signal. They sank their teeth into the dam's branches and yanked them free.

As the animals cheered and the water flowed, Seven hoped that her plan would work.

The water flowed from the lake down into the tunnels, filling up the sinkholes with sticky, gooey mud. The first thing the next morning, a human stepped in one up to his knees.

"What the!" he exclaimed. A co-worker helped him up. "What is that?"

As they walked closer to the trees, they noticed that the ground felt spongy underfoot. "Something's not right," said another human.

Seven, Arni, Fig, and Merriweather watched the crew

as they walked all over the area, poking sticks down into the soil and, once in a while, falling down in a heap when the ground collapsed beneath their feet. They summoned a large human, who stomped about, shouting and waving his arms. An argument ensued, and although they could not make out the exact meaning, the animals understood well enough: The ground was no longer good for building.

Had they not been so busy shouting at one another, the humans would have heard a curious thing: a chorus of chirps, squeaks, and yips—the sound of the forest folk celebrating.

"You can stay, you know," Fig said to Seven as they watched Arnica and five young bunnies play tag in the sunshine on the hilltop. "We're safe now."

Seven shook her head. "I'm glad I could help. But this isn't the place we need to be."

Merriweather looked sage. "You have a larger mission, do you not?"

Seven replied, "I know a little, based on what our grandfather told me. There is a place of safety, where humans can't go. I want to take Arni there, and I want to find my mother and brother, and bring them there, too." She hesitated, but when she saw the knowing gleam in the owl's eyes, she said, "And you know I am needed there."

"We owls are not the most musical of the birdfolk," Merriweather admitted, "but we do love rhyme. And the rhyme I learned beneath my mother's wing told that the Notch is a place safe for all creatures. But that one day it would face a great danger. And only one creature—a seven-ringed raccoon who had been born when the moon was copper—would be able to gather together bird and beast to stave off the threat."

"That didn't rhyme," Fig pointed out.

"My mother had a gift for rhyme. Me, not so much." Merriweather clacked his bill warmly. "You are the one who will save the Notch and all its creatures, whether they live there now or have yet to make their journey. Consider what you have done for us here a practice run, young friend. I wish you fair weather and soft grass beneath your feet."

Fig touched her nose to Seven's. "We will keep watch for your mother and brother, I promise. If they come by here, we will send them after you. I'm sure you'll be together before long."

Chapter 9

North of the woods lay the houses of people. They were not as close together as the buildings in the city had been but instead were separated by swaths of green grass, long skinny parking lots ("Driveways," Brangwy explained), and swimming pools. Merriweather advised them to travel either at night or in late morning, when humans were least likely to be about. "Humans here start their days early," the owl had explained.

Seven, Arnica, and Brangwy started out the next day. Their first morning away from the woods found them in the middle of a driveway when the garage door began to lift. The grinding, clanking sound reminded Seven and Arnica of the yellow monster, and they raced away in case the house was hungry for raccoons.

Many homes had large bushes in the front, and their

thick branches provided good hiding spots. Yet the sisters could not hide completely; a dog caught their scent through an open window and launched itself at the screen, barking furiously until its human screamed at it to stop.

Arnica said, "That's sad. Dog's only doing its job."

Seven-Rings nodded.

"I'm thirsty," Arnica said.

"Me too," Seven said.

"And hungry," Arni added.

Seven's stomach growled in answer. But where could they find food? This place had no broken pavement with puddles of water—no leaves, seeds, or discarded wrappers in the gutters, no trash cans or dumpsters.

From below a bush, Seven asked Brangwy, "Can you help us find something to eat?"

In answer, Brangwy picked up a pebble and dropped it, uncomfortable with what she was going to say. "The gardens I have seen have no good veggies. There is something, although I don't know if you will like it."

"Anything!" Seven said. Arni nodded in agreement.

"Follow me, then," Brangwy said. The crow flapped her strong wings and lifted off the ground effortlessly, landing a little way down the road on a fire hydrant. The sister raccoons hurried to keep up with her, and it became a game of sorts. As soon as they drew within a few yards, the crow would take off again and fly another little distance. Over and over they did this, for most of the day, until Seven's sensitive nose caught a scent.

Seven and Arnica walked to the edge of a concrete clearing. On the far side, they saw a slender cat eating out of a bowl.

The cat saw them, too, but to their surprise, it didn't hiss or growl. Instead, it sat down and greeted them cheerfully. "Hey there, strangers!" the cat said. "There's plenty, if you're hungry."

Seven and Arnica darted out of the shrubs toward the cat. A sudden shriek from inside the house startled them, and they dashed back for cover.

Suddenly, the cat charged into the bush behind them. Seven-Rings hissed and puffed up her fur. "Easy! Easy!" said the cat, who sat down nonchalantly and began licking her left forepaw. "I'm only keeping up appearances."

Seven, standing between the cat and her little sister, stopped hissing. "What does that mean?"

The cat explained, "My owner expects me to chase off creatures like you, who aren't doing a bit of harm." The cat shook her head. "I don't know what she'd do if she saw some of the less-nice creatures that come around. That's when I go inside." The cat's ears swiveled toward the house as she said, "We'll wait a bit, and she'll forget all about you."

"My name is Seven. This is my sister, Arnica. We're

from the city, and we're heading north."

The cat cocked her head. "You've come a long way already."

"We've been traveling for a while. At least three moon cycles, maybe more. I've lost count," Seven admitted.

"When you're busy trying to stay in one piece, I imagine that you don't think much about the passage of time," the cat said kindly. "I'm a human pet. We don't have much to worry about. Our days are very, very long."

"You live with people?" Seven asked, surprised.

"Oh, yes. I've been with this family ever since I was a kitten. I spend most of my time inside."

Seven shook her head in amazement. "We lived in an old church. The people didn't use it anymore. We played with the things they left behind and slept on an old couch."

"I love couches!" the cat said. "But laps are even better." She turned her head toward the house. "They'll be eating dinner soon, and while they do, help yourselves to my bowl. If they make a move to come outside, I'll run out first so that you can hide. OK?"

With the plan set, Seven and Arnica watched the cat saunter back to the house and enter through the pet door. They waited a few moments, listening to the chatter of voices and the clatter of dishes from inside the house. Then they hurried over to the bowl and devoured the crunchy food, stuffing one morsel into their mouths with one paw while picking up another with the other paw. They emptied the bowl and scampered back beneath the bush.

The night grew dark, and lights came on in the houses around them. Seven heard the pet door open, and soon the cat joined them under the bush. "I'm glad to see you ate up."

"Thanks for that, but where are the dumpsters?" Seven asked.

The cat chuckled. "None of those around here, I'm afraid. The people in this town like things just so." She shrugged. "They're odd, but I love them." Suddenly the cat's eyes grew wide. "Oh, my manners! I never introduced myself. My name is Isabelle, although that's not what my people call me. They call me Mrs. Whiskers." She closed her eyes and sighed at the ridiculousness of the name. "As I said, they're odd. But why don't you come inside for a little while? I've got someone I want you to meet."

As Seven-Rings and Arnica followed Isabelle toward the house, Isabelle paused in mid-step to sniff the night air. Seven could smell something, too. She didn't recognize the scent, but it made her fur stand on end. "Quick! In the house!" Isabelle said. Seven pushed Arnica along after Isabelle. The pet door, picking up the signal from a sensor on Isabelle's collar, unlatched itself, and the three of them tumbled inside.

"What's that smell?" Seven-Rings asked.

Eyes wide and pupils round, Isabelle answered, "Coyote."

The coyote appeared like a ghost out of the darkness beyond the glass door. It had long legs and a sharply pointed nose that twitched as it caught their scent. It opened its mouth in a predatory smile to show sharp white teeth. Its eyes were bright with the thrill of the hunt.

"Missed you this time, cat, but I'll get you in the end."

The coyote's voice was rough and raw, as if speaking was painful. "I'll get your visitors, too. It's been a long while since I've eaten raccoon. A personal favorite of mine."

Arnica began to tremble, and Seven felt her fur rise with anger. She blurted, "You won't eat us."

"Oh, no? Big talk from a small mammal. I've eaten mice bigger than you."

"Not anymore you won't," she said. "I'm going to stop you."

The coyote chuckled. "You're going to stop me? You and that stub-tailed reject from a trap? You can't think that you can actually best me. I'll snap your neck when you least expect it." The coyote turned away, lifted his leg, and shot a stream of yellow urine down the glass door. Chuckling at his own rude joke, he trotted away to find another creature to terrify.

Isabelle shook her elegant head. "You shouldn't have talked to him like that."

Her fur still puffed out, Seven remembered the battle between Greyson and the dog. "Nasty dog," she hissed.

Isabelle cocked her head. "Yes, they're related to dogs. I'd forgotten that."

"Dogs are evil," Seven said.

"No, not all of them," Isabelle said. "That one is, well, confused, I think. Dogs don't like to live alone; they need to be in a family. Well, we all need family, but dogs especially.

Come on, I'll introduce you to a dog that's anything but evil."

Quietly, they followed Isabelle into the kitchen, through a forest of table and chair legs, and into a room filled with worn, comfortable furniture that smelled strongly of people. "They use this room a lot," Isabelle explained. "The dining room, which we just came through, gets used twice a year." She meowed softly. "Lucius! Are you awake?"

A groan escaped from the couch, and a massive head appeared. "What is it, Izzy?" Seven's mouth fell open. The coyote had been huge, but this dog—this dog was immense! His head alone was as big as her whole body. Yet his eyes glowed with kindness.

Isabelle leaped onto the couch and began to knead at the furry side. "Lucius raised me from a kitten," she said, as the Newfoundland gave her an affectionate lick. To Lucius, she said, "This is Seven-Rings and Arnica. We got in just before that dreadful coyote came."

The dog sneezed in disapproval. "That piece of trash! I could rid the neighborhood of him right quick."

"Why don't you?" asked Seven.

Isabelle said, "The coyote comes around at night, when our people have locked Lucius inside."

The dog rose to his feet. "And I certainly can't fit through the pet door," the big dog said. Seven looked him right in the knee. He looked down at her benevolently. "It's good to see that you aren't afraid just because I'm big," he said. "Many creatures—and some people—see only my size. They don't get to know me."

Arnica crept up and touched the big dog's leg. He nosed her affectionately. "Care for a ride?" Without hesitation, she clambered up onto the huge dog's back. Seven and Isabelle followed the giant dog out of the den and into the kitchen. Arnica squeaked very softly as she swung gently from side to side on the Newfoundland's back.

Chapter 10

After Lucius got a drink from a bowl that seemed to Seven only a little smaller than the concrete pond outside, the four animals lay in a congenial circle on the kitchen floor. Isabelle departed occasionally to make sure the humans, whom she called Fitzsimmonses, were still asleep. She needn't have worried. Snores drifted down the stairs from the second floor.

Seven listened curiously as Isabelle and Lucius described the life of a pet. "The humans give us food and water, and keep us safe from the weather and other things," Isabelle explained.

Seven was confused. "Why do they do that?"

"We give them friendship, just as we would any other member of a pack," Lucius said.

"I prefer to think of it as a family," sniffed Isabelle.

"Yes, Izzy—a family," said Lucius. "The humans are in charge, of course."

Isabelle grinned mischievously. "Or so they think."

Lucius gave another thunderous chuckle. "That's true.

This little cat has had them wrapped around her paw since they found her at the shelter."

"Shel-ter?" asked Arni.

Lucius said, "That's a place where—well, it's hard to explain."

Isabelle sat up and licked a paw, trying to hide her discomfort at the conversation's turn. "You see, there are more pets than people," she explained. "The extra pets wait in shelters. Some are lucky and get adopted."

Arnica said, "They get families!" Lucius licked her, and she was bowled over. She squeaked with delight.

"What about the unlucky ones?" asked Seven. The dog and cat exchanged uncomfortable looks. "What happens to them?" Seven insisted.

Finally, Lucius said, "They get put to sleep."

Seven said, "What does that mean?"

"When a pet gets old or gets really sick and will soon die, the humans give it a needle."

"Like a sewing needle?" Seven asked, utterly confused. She had once found a box of the unpleasant sharp objects in the old ladies' parlor, and Runner had explained that humans had used them to make things out of cloth. How a sewing needle would help an animal was beyond Seven's imagination.

"No, dear," said Lucius, in a voice so soft that it reminded her of distant thunder on a warm evening. "It's medicine. It stops their heart."

Seven covered Arnica's ears. "You mean—they kill them?"

Cat and dog nodded sadly. "Sometimes it happens because the pet is ill. Remember Georgie?" Lucius said to Isabelle. "He lived next door. He was very old and very sick, and it was time for him to rest. That's when getting a needle is not so bad. But in other places, at other times, the animals are, well, in the way. Humans try to find homes for all of us, but it isn't always possible."

Arni shook her head free from her sister's paws and gave Seven a sour look. Yet Seven was more concerned with what she had just heard. "Why can't these other pets live in the wild?" she asked.

"We don't remember how," Isabelle explained. "We've lived with people for thousands of years. We don't remember the wild ways. I catch bugs and mice, but I don't think I'm good enough to keep myself fed."

"The people are my pack," added Lucius. "I need them as much as they need me."

Suddenly, the animals heard human footsteps overhead. Isabelle leaped to her feet. "Mom's up. We'd better get you out of here."

Lucius rose on his massive paws, looking like a truck standing up. "Under the front porch," he said to Isabelle.

"Great idea!" the cat said. To Seven and Arnica, she

said, "You can stay under the front steps. They won't see you."

"I'll slow Mom down while you get our visitors out. Until tonight, my dears!" He bounded up the stairs to greet his family in a manner enthusiastic enough to delay their arrival on the first floor.

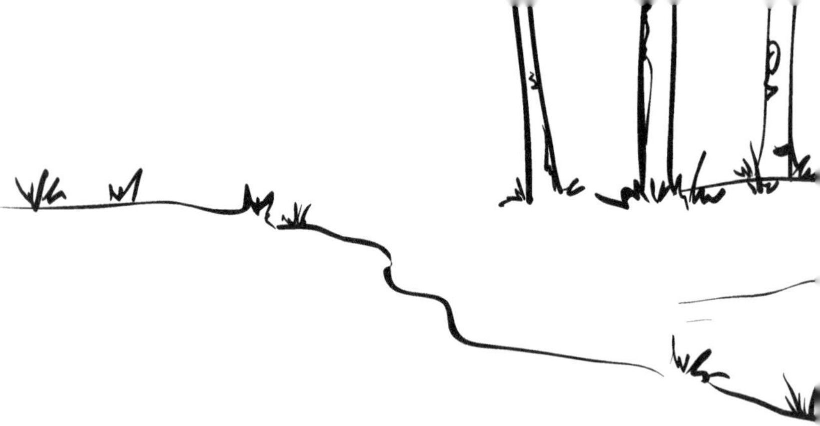

CHAPTER 11

Isabelle led the raccoons out through the cat door, around the side of the house, and to a sheltered spot under the front steps. "You'll be safe here," the cat said. "I'll bring you some food later on." They thanked her, and she disappeared back the way they had come.

Under the stairs it was quiet and dark. The bare earth felt soft and cool below their paws, and its smell comforted Seven. Three months of living in the wild had made her uncomfortable in human places, although she had lived in a human place most of her life. She stretched out, rubbing herself into the cool soil and delighting in the way it felt against her fur and skin. Arnica snuggled up to Seven. "Nice dog," she said sleepily.

A loud thumping overhead woke Seven after what seemed to be just a minute of sleep. She slipped out from beneath Arnica and peered out. A small human, with large green feet and a bright yellow coat, was jumping up and down on the grass. A slightly larger human said, "I don't know why you want to wear your boots. Mom said it's not gonna rain."

The smaller human replied, "I like my boots. And you never know."

Two more thumps startled Seven, and she shrank back under the porch. One of the thumps, in a voice older than the other two smallish humans, said, "Don't forget, you both have soccer after school, so do not take the bus home. Only Jenni is coming home on the bus."

"Yes, Mom," the boot wearer and her older sister said.

Mom and the fourth thump came into view. She was a tiny human, the smallest of the three, and she wore a backpack that looked—Seven gasped—like a raccoon! At first she thought it might be real, but then she saw that the fur was fake and the eyes were plastic. She relaxed, and her own fur laid flat again.

Mom, the small human Jenni, the boot wearer (whose name was Martha), and the older sister (whose name was Brooke) all stood near the road. Occasionally, Martha and Jenni tore away from the others to chase each other around. Brooke fussed at them until her mother assured her that it was OK. "But why can't they just wait, like normal people?"

Mom hugged Brooke. "It's tough being the big sister, isn't it?"

Seven felt a catch in her throat. It was, indeed.

Around the bend in the street came an enormous yellow vehicle, and when she first saw it, Seven thought it was the monster that had devoured the church. But as she watched, the three smaller humans climbed into it. With a sigh, it swallowed them up and moved away. Mom waved as the vehicle departed, then thumped up the steps again and went back into the house.

Torn between curiosity about what the humans were doing and her desire to remain hidden, Seven left the shelter of the stairs and climbed into the thickly leaved rhododendron bush. From within its foliage, she could peer into the window. From her vantage point, she could see Mom and another large human drinking from cups in the kitchen.

Isabelle jumped onto the windowsill. Startled, Seven almost tumbled out of the rhododendron. "I thought you'd be asleep," whispered the cat.

"I was curious," Seven said.

"They are fascinating, aren't they?" Isabelle said.

While the animals watched, the other large human (who, Isabelle explained, was known as either "Dad," "Honey," or, less commonly, "Bruce") rinsed the breakfast dishes and placed them in a metal box. Then Mom (who was known as "Angie" or "Honey," though it was rather confusing why she and her mate had the same name) took

Lucius outside. "One last chance for him to pee before they leave," Isabelle explained.

Seven wrinkled her nose at the idea of having one's toileting schedule dictated by humans.

Morning chores done, Honey and Honey prepared to leave the house. They vanished from Seven's view, and within a moment, she heard two car doors slam and garage doors begin to grind their way open. The adults, each in a separate car, backed out of the garage and into the street. Silence soon settled over the neighborhood.

"There won't be much else to see," Isabelle admitted. "Most of the humans around here are gone all day to work or school. Mom will come back around 3:00 p.m. to meet the bus, and then things will be noisy and interesting until bedtime."

"What do you do until then?"

Lucius said, "Usually we sleep. But why don't you all come in and you can explore some more."

Arni was waiting under the stairs, eyes bright with the thought of going inside.

"Are you OK, Arni?" Seven asked.

"I'm hungry!" Arnica announced.

When they got inside, Isabelle rose effortlessly to the counter. "What would you like?" She opened a cabinet that was full of boxes and bags, and Seven could smell their contents from where she stood. The food here was not on the outside of the buildings, but on the inside. "You can try anything, as long as it's not in a metal can. Even Lucius can't open one of those." She knocked a white bag out of the cabinet to the counter, and then to the floor. "You might like those," Isabelle said. "The girls do."

Seven unfolded the top of the bag and reached in to draw out a small object. It was larger than the bits of dry cat food and smelled familiar. "Cheese!" Seven said. She bit into the cracker and was rewarded with a cheesy crunch. As she chewed happily, she handed one to Arnica.

"Try one of these," Isabelle said. She knocked a black-and-white cookie to the floor. "The girls love them, too."

Seven bit into the cookie, and the sweetness erupted in her mouth. She coughed in surprise.

Isabelle picked various things out, including a breadstick, which was delicious, and a spongy yellow cake with white frosting, which was very sweet. Seven sampled each treat, exclaiming over the new flavors. Then she realized that Arnica was not eating. Instead, she was gazing at one of the shiny brass handles on the kitchen cabinet, the fish-shaped cracker in her paws.

Isabelle and Lucius had noticed it, too. "Is she all right?" Lucius asked, his voice a soft rumble.

"She gets very still when she's thinking hard about something," Seven said. "Give her a moment."

"Seven," the small raccoon finally said. "When will the nasty dog come back?"

"The coyote?"

Isabelle said, "He comes every two days."

"He's a bully," Arnica said matter-of-factly. "Seven, you need to help."

"What do you mean?"

Arnica looked at the cracker and appeared surprised to see it. "You need to make the coyote go away. Like you stopped the houses from coming to the lake."

"Arni, I didn't really . . ." Seven began, but then she stopped to think. "If we could get Lucius out of the house when the coyote comes, then he could scare it away."

Isabelle shook her head. "But Lucius is too big to fit through the pet door."

"And the family always locks up before bed." Lucius stood up and shook himself.

Seven's mind began to whir. She had been able to open every latch in the old church. Perhaps there was a way . . .

The sudden clanking of the garage door startled all four animals. "They're home?" Isabelle squeaked. "Why are they home? Quick, you have to get out." She leaped off the counter and raced to the pet door, Arnica and Seven close behind. Lucius gave the kitchen floor one more lick and then hurried to the door that led from the garage into the kitchen. The key turned in the lock as Seven ducked through the door. She heard Honey/Bruce's voice say, "Good boy, Lucius! Down, boy! Down!" and one of the girls comment, "He must know I don't feel good, Dad."

Safely beneath the steps, Isabelle touched noses with the sisters and returned to the house. Now it was Arni's turn to ask her sister, "What are you thinking about?"

Seven replied, "I think I have a way to get rid of the coyote for good."

Chapter 12

The next night, Seven and Arnica crept to the edge of the concrete clearing behind the house, staying far enough away to be safe but close enough to see in through the glass doors. The family had finished their dinner, and the girls were sitting at the table, heads bent over their books.

Isabelle was sitting on the chair, her paws tucked under her chest, doing an excellent imitation of a loaf of bread. Her ear twitched, and she glanced up to spy Seven's eyes, two bright circles outdoors reflecting the light from the kitchen. Nonchalantly, the cat leaped down from the chair, stretched, and sauntered outdoors.

To Seven, she said, "It's early yet. They're all still awake."

Seven nodded. "I know. But when they go to bed, I need to get in as quickly as possible."

The cat agreed before she vanished indoors once again. Seven and Arnica tucked themselves in between a wooden outdoor chair and the wall of the house and watched the moon rise.

"Do you remember the moon story?" Arni asked softly.

Seven searched her memory. "I do," Seven said. "That was the only time we'd ever heard of a coyote before now, isn't it?"

"Tell me the story, while we wait," Arni said.

Seven cleared her throat and began. "When the world was new, First Coyote was the newest of the First Animals, having just been created by the Big Paw. He was so excited to be alive! He jumped and barked, annoying his big brother Wolf, cousin Fox, and pretty much everybody else—including the moon. But First Coyote thought that the moon was the most glorious thing in the world, and every night, when the moon rose, First Coyote sang a song to impress the moon. Although Moon tried again and again to ask First Coyote to be quiet, First Coyote couldn't hear Moon's voice over his own singing. So Moon turned away, and the sky went dark.

"The other First Animals were frightened that First Coyote had driven Moon away. Seeing at night was almost impossible without Moon's help. So First Possum decided to take matters into his own paws. He went to First Coyote and told him that Moon would only come back if First

Coyote climbed to the top of the tallest pine and apologized. First Coyote was sad that he had made the moon disappear, so he agreed.

"Unlike First Possum, First Coyote was not a tree climber. He struggled up the tree. Possum had a terrible plan in mind: He was going to make First Coyote fall out of the tree. 'Is this high enough?' First Coyote asked. First Possum shook his head and said that he had to go all the way to the top.

"It was very quiet, and the moon could hear First Coyote's nervous whining as he went higher and higher. Finally, First Coyote crept out onto the highest branch, while First Possum snickered, 'No more howling for you!' That's when the branches snapped under First Coyote's weight. He fell, howling with fear, sure he would die. But the moon had seen First Possum's cruel trick. It sent down a moonbeam to catch First Coyote, letting him slide safely down to earth.

"First Coyote howled to the moon to say thank you for saving his life, and he does so even today."

"And I bet that Possum watches his step," said Isabelle, who had silently joined them. "And I doubt our coyote has been saved by a moonbeam," the cat said drily. "Everyone's asleep. Are you ready?"

"Stay here, Arni," Seven said. "You should be safe here."

As they walked to the pet door, Isabelle kept looking over her shoulder. Seven said, "Don't worry. Our plan will work."

"I just don't want anybody to get hurt," the cat said.

"If this works the way I think it will, that coyote won't hurt anyone again," Seven said.

Inside, Lucius was waiting for them. Seven-Rings could hear the big dog's heart thumping as she asked, "You're sure you can do this?" Lucius nodded, not trusting himself to speak.

Carefully, Seven climbed up onto the dog's back. She worked quietly on the door latch. With a soft snap, it opened, but it didn't budge, not even when Lucius gripped the handle with his mouth and tugged it sideways. "Wait!" said Seven. She saw the problem: A thick wooden stick lay in the door's track and kept it from moving. She pulled up one end, and Isabelle rolled it away. Lucius tried the door again. It slid open with a whisper.

Lucius trembled with excitement. "I should go outside," he said.

Seven put her paws on the big dog's chest. "No. If he sees or smells you he won't come near. You need to stay here."

Isabelle crossed in front of Seven. "This isn't your fight, Seven. I should go."

"No, Isabelle. It's my plan. I'm going to be the bait."

With that, Seven slipped out the open door and padded to the center of the patio. She curled up in a ball, feigning sleep. Crickets chirruped in the grass and the bushes. Normally, they would have lulled her to sleep, but tonight was anything but normal.

Then a hush fell. A strong musty smell tickled her nose. Her skin prickled. The coyote was near. She heard his nails click on the concrete. With a thunderous bark, Lucius cannoned out of the open door and hit the coyote square, knocking him to the side.

Seven leaped into a shrub and watched. Snarling, dog and coyote snapped at each other. Lights came on inside the house. Seven heard human voices and shrank further into the shrub. The patio light shattered the darkness, momentarily blinding all the animals. "Bruce, call the police!" shouted the woman. "Lucius caught that coyote!"

"Don't—need—help!" snarled Lucius. He grabbed the coyote by the back of the neck.

The coyote yelped, "Don't kill me!"

"Give me one reason why I shouldn't!" Lucius said. "I can snap your neck with one bite!"

"Lucius! Don't hurt him!" Seven called from the bush.

"He's a killer!" Lucius growled.

"But you aren't," Seven said. She stepped out from her hiding place to look the big dog in the eye. Dangling from Lucius's jaws, the coyote rolled his own fear-filled eyes to her. A siren wailed in the distance.

Fighting his instincts, which were urging him to eliminate the threat once and for all, Lucius growled to the coyote, "Will you leave and never come back?"

"Yes, yes, I will!" whimpered the coyote.

Lucius said, "Swear it by the Big Paw." The coyote hesitated. Lucius shook him. "Swear!"

"I swear! I swear by the Big Paw!" yelped the coyote. Lucius opened his jaws, and the coyote ran across the concrete clearing, jumped over a bush, and was gone.

The woman, wearing a T-shirt and sweatpants, ran out to Lucius. "Oh, Lucius, are you all right?" Isabelle tiptoed out of the house and rubbed against the big dog and then against the woman. The man and the three little humans came out of the house and patted the Newfoundland's massive head. "Good job, big guy! Good boy!" Lucius wagged his tail madly at the praise.

"But—how did he open the door?" the woman asked.

The humans shared a puzzled look, and then the man said, "I must have forgotten to lock it." From the safety of her shrub, Seven harrumphed.

The police arrived. Seven watched the officers take notes and tell the family to take Lucius to the vet for a checkup. "The vet!" he groused to Isabelle. "That wasn't part of the plan."

"Mama! Look what I found!" called the littlest girl. She entered the circle of people, cuddling Arnica in her arms.

"Oh, no!" Seven exclaimed.

Arnica was not frightened; she was half asleep. "Don't move, honey!" the woman said.

"Can I see that, sweetheart?" one of the officers asked gently. He reached out and took Arnica from the child.

The other officer said, "I better call Faye and Colin."

Seven-Rings asked, "What is Fayeandcolin?"

Isabelle answered, "They take injured animals away in a truck."

"What happens then?" Seven demanded.

Isabelle's whiskers drooped. "I'm sorry. I don't know."

The officer said, "Faye says she'll be right along."

Seven tried not to panic. Someone was going to take Arnica away in a truck, to an unknown fate. Somehow, she had to find a way to go with her sister. She turned to Isabelle. "Bite me."

"Beg pardon?" Isabelle said.

"Bite my leg, hard. Make me bleed. Wherever they're taking Arnica, I have to go, too," she explained urgently.

"OK," said the cat. And she bit.

The pain raced up Seven's foreleg like fire and made her feel queasy. She'd never had an injury of any sort. If this was a quarter of the pain Arni had experienced when the pike bit her—

"Sorry." Isabelle licked the raccoon on the forehead, fondly. "We can't thank you enough."

Bleeding from Isabelle's well-placed chomp, Seven limped out of the shrub, crying loudly. "Look! Another one!" said the man.

"The coyote must have been after them," said one of the officers.

"That one's hurt," observed the littlest girl.

There came the sound of a truck pulling into the driveway. "Back here, Faye," called one of the officers.

The woman named Faye had short brown hair, glasses, and a stocky build. "Had a bit of excitement around here, did you?" she said. When everyone nodded, she walked over to Lucius and petted him on the head. "Good job, big guy! Good boy! What have you got there, David?"

In answer, the police officer handed Arnica over. "Well, aren't you just a wee bit of a thing," the wildlife rescuer said.

"There's another one there. The coyote bit her," said the officer.

"OK, keep your eyes on her. Let me put this one in the truck."

Seven-Rings's heart pounded as she watched the woman carry her sister off to the pickup truck and place her in a pet carrier. She did not move as the wildlife rescuer approached. "You need some help, sweetheart?" the woman said softly.

Just as Lucius had to fight his urge to kill the coyote, Seven had to fight her urge to flee. Shaking, she allowed herself to be picked up. She closed her eyes and endured being carried to the truck. The woman placed her gently into a plastic pet carrier and clicked the door shut. As the woman closed the liftgate, Seven heard Lucius howl, "Best of luck, Little Brave Ones!"

Chapter 13

The musk of woodchuck, the whisper of fox, the faint odor of feathers filled the truck. Strongest, however, was the smell of the plastic pet carrier she rode in.

Seven pressed her face against the slots in the side and peered out. Although it was dark, she could see the other carrier. "Arni! Arni!" she called. There was no response.

Worried, she licked at the wound on her leg and waited helplessly to see what would happen next. The truck finally slowed and stopped. Seven heard the driver's door open and shut, and footsteps crunch on gravel. The back of the truck opened, and Seven squinted against the floodlight that streamed in. "Come on, you two, let's get you taken care of," said the woman.

The plastic box swayed as the woman carried it, and Seven slithered across the smooth plastic bottom, banging into the side and jolting her leg painfully. She mewled in protest. "Sorry!" said the woman. "Clumsy of me. I'll try to do better."

Seven felt her carrier set down on the floor, near the legs of a metal examination table. Steel cages lined the walls. Seven could smell other animals. In a cage directly across from her lay a magnificent red fox, who was awake and watching the proceedings with interest.

Suddenly, a large cat appeared outside the door of Seven's carrier. With a start, Seven realized it was a bobcat. She shrank back into the cage, trembling. The bobcat saw her reaction. "Don't worry," he purred. "I don't eat wild food."

The fox said, "I don't think she believes you."

Just then the woman returned. "Greeting our new customers, are you, Bobby?" she said to the bobcat.

"Yes," he replied, which to the human sounded like "Rowr."

Astonished, Seven said, "You can talk to humans?"

The bobcat said, "Her vocabulary is pretty limited, but she's a good sort. Practically an animal herself. She saved me when I was a kitten, and so I've been here ever since. Going on five winters now."

"What is she going to do?" Seven-Rings asked, as the woman took things out of a drawer and placed them on a metal tray.

"She's going to check you over and mend your leg," said Bobby.

"Then put you in a cage," said the fox.

Bobby licked one massive paw, unperturbed by the snarky remark. "For a little while. You know that, Evangeline. You've been here before."

The animals fell silent as the woman picked up Seven's carrier. She placed it on the metal table and opened the front door. "Come on, lovey, let's get a look at you."

Seven-Rings hesitated. From the floor, Bobby said, "Don't make her shake you out. She will, you know."

Seven took the cat's advice. She crept out onto the smooth metal table. She had never been this close to a human before, and the face that loomed above her was pink and hairless, no whiskers at all, with blue eyes that had a white background that gave them a wild look. The woman smiled and showed square white teeth. Seven looked away in fear. "It's OK, little one. Let's check you over, shall we?"

Although there was no pain, being touched made Seven shudder. The woman tipped her this way and that, peered in her ears, looked under her tail. "You seem pretty healthy, except for that bite," she said. "Looks like a cat bite—way too small for a coyote and not very deep. Looks like the cat didn't really mean it."

She placed Seven on a scale, which bobbed beneath her. The woman then returned Seven to the carrier and took a few moments to make scratching noises on a sheet of white paper, like the kind Seven and Typhoo loved tearing up in the old church. "Let me check out your friend here, and then we'll take care of that wound."

As Seven watched her put the box containing Arnica on the table, the door to the clinic opened. "Need any help?" said a man.

"This one's sleepy and a little underweight. Somehow she lost most of her tail. Poor little thing. Would you prep a couple of cages for me?" the woman said.

The man moved quietly around the wildlife clinic, filling water bowls and placing newspaper and towels into two cages. The woman placed Arnica into a cage on the top tier, above and to the left of the fox.

"What about this one?" the man asked.

"Leg wound. Do you want to hold or dress?"

In answer, the man pulled on a pair of thick gloves. He was just as gentle as the woman had been. Carefully, the woman drew Seven's leg straight and washed it well. As the woman bandaged the wound, the man asked, "Do you need a collar?"

"Let's put one on for tonight. I don't think she'll need it for long." The woman went to another drawer and took out another smelly piece of plastic. This she fastened around Seven's neck. "There you go," the woman said, her voice echoing painfully in the cone around Seven's head.

The man put her in a cage, and then the humans left. The clinic was quiet and dark.

The bobcat padded silently over to her cage.

"Where are we?" Seven asked.

"St. Francis Wildlife Rehabilitation Center. Faye and Colin are the people who run it. They take in wounded and orphaned creatures."

"I'm no orphan," said Evangeline, crossly.

"No, but you sure got messed up by that bird shot," Bobby answered. He turned to Seven. "She's just embarrassed. Colin had to shave her butt to get the pellets out. Until her fur grows back, she's a three-quarters red, one-quarter pink fox."

The other creatures in the cages erupted with laughter. Seven-Rings jumped, for she hadn't realized they had been listening. Grumbling, the fox curled up on the towel in her cage, her back to the rest of them.

"Now, Evangeline," said an elderly beaver across the room. "Don't take it personally."

"She'll be fine," said Bobby. "She knows I'm only kidding." The fox was silent.

Seven-Rings said, "Please, sir, can you tell me how my sister is?"

"Sir, is it? Don't be so formal, youngster. Plain old Bobby's fine with me." Obligingly, the bobcat leaped from the floor to the table to the top of the cages. He peered into Arnica's cage. "Sleeping, it looks like. Seems that she ate everything they gave her, and now she's out cold." He jumped straight down to the floor.

"I have to get her. We have to get out."

Bobby said, "Why?"

"Why?" Seven tried to reach through the bars, but the cone prevented her. She twisted this way and that. When she could reach the latch, she couldn't see, and when she could see, she couldn't reach the latch. She growled in frustration. "Humans are trouble, don't you know that?"

"She's young but smart!" groused the vixen.

"Some of them are, but some of them aren't," Bobby said gently. "They just want to help you. Your sister's got the right idea. Sleep. You're safe. And everything will look brighter in the morning." With that, he padded away.

Seven resigned herself to doing nothing more. She closed her eyes and, in the darkness and quiet, fell asleep.

Chapter 14

Seven woke when she heard the door open. The woman, Faye, came over to her cage and said, "And how are you this morning?"

Seven hissed at her.

The woman said, "OK, I understand. We need to take a look at that leg. But with your temper, I think you're a two-person patient. I'll wait for Colin. Let me see how your little friend is doing."

Seven watched as the woman took Arnica out of her cage. The tiny raccoon sat on the metal table and allowed the woman to look at her closely, even at her tail. "Now, I wonder what happened to make you lose such a pretty tail? What was it, huh?"

Arnica said, "Big fish," although to Faye she merely seemed to chirrup.

"Is that so?" Faye continued as she examined the stub. "Well, it certainly healed well. You must have a good doctor."

"I have a good sister," said Arnica, which sounded like more chirps to the human.

Faye chuckled warmly. "You certainly are the little chatterbox, aren't you?" she said. In reply, Arnica climbed up onto the woman's shoulder and licked her ear.

Seven cried, "Arni! What are you doing?"

Arnica replied, "I like her. She makes me happy."

"She's a human! Her kind destroyed our home! Don't you remember?" Seven said.

Arnica didn't answer, but began to investigate the woman's hair. Faye laughed.

Seven shrieked, "Arni! Don't!"

Bobby materialized outside of Seven's cage. "Don't worry."

"You don't understand!" Seven snapped, fear making her angry. "She's . . . she's . . ." Words failed her. "I have to take care of her," she finished.

"Do you? Seems to me that she knows what she needs," the bobcat replied with a yawn.

"She can't!" Seven-Rings said.

The cat's eyes glittered. "How do you know?"

She stopped and watched her sister, who was creeping across the woman's shoulders, clinging with her claws but being careful not to scratch. The woman said, "My goodness, you're a real love bug, aren't you?"

The man came in and saw the tiny raccoon on his wife's shoulders. "Uh, oh," he said.

"This one's special, Colin."

"Like Bobby?"

"Well, Bobby's mostly lazy. He can't be bothered to go back to the wild." At that, the cat huffed indignantly into his whiskers. "This one, she's been through a lot already. Yet she's very sweet," the woman added.

Recognizing a good opportunity, Arnica reached forward and grasped the man's shirtsleeve. Then she pulled herself up to his shoulder.

Seven-Rings hid her eyes. "No, no," she whispered.

Bobby purred with amusement. "Why are you so upset?" he asked.

"Because we can't stay. There's something—something important I have to do." She looked up at Bobby pleadingly. "You know, don't you?"

Suddenly solemn, the cat nodded. "We've talked about it here, among ourselves, wondering if the prophecy is true. Even creatures who will never go to the Notch know of the terrible threat. The bats have seen it themselves, and told me. They say that there is now a road for trucks and construction equipment leading right up to the very edge of the Notch. Soon the gift of the First Animals will be no

more." The sparkle returned to his eyes unexpectedly. "Unless, of course, there is someone with a seven-ringed tail who happened to be born under a copper moon somewhere in the vicinity, who is brave and clever."

Softly, Seven said, "I can do it."

The fox yawned hugely, showing that she didn't believe a word. "Raccoons are the most ridiculous dreamers. Humans are everywhere. There's no place you can go where there aren't people. This Notch place is no different."

"It is so!" Seven shot back. "The Notch is a place for us, the furred and feathered. First Raccoon promised."

"Fool!" the fox retorted. "There is no such place!"

"Liar!" Seven snarled.

A growl from Bobby silenced them both. "Behave yourselves," he ordered. "We are talking about the other raccoon."

Seven's mouth opened as she saw Arnica riding around on the man's shoulders as he did his chores. Seven could hear her contented squeaks.

"Oh, Arni," she whispered.

"Come on, Bobby, move over," said the man as he approached Seven's cage. Slowly, as if moving were entirely his own idea, the cat stepped aside. The man opened the front of Seven's cage. "Let's take a look at you, OK? I think we can take that collar off," he said.

She hesitated. Arnica, perched on the man's shoulders, said, "Come on, Seven! He's good. Not like the big fish."

Her sister's words reassured her, and so, despite her misgivings, she let the man pick her up. "That's the way!" he said softly to her. Then he addressed Arnica, "You know, you're a great little assistant." She chirruped with delight.

The examination was quick and gentle. The man changed the bandage. True to his word, he removed the protective collar from around Seven's neck.

Carefully, Arnica scrambled down the man's arm to sniff her sister. She said, "Oh, Seven, I was worried."

"I was worried about you, too, Arni."

"Did it hurt?"

"The bite? Only a little. It looked worse than it was." Seven touched the bandage with her paw. "They really know how to fix things here. I wish we'd known them when we met the big fish." She shuddered. "What's going to happen to us?" she asked aloud.

From the floor, Bobby said. "Don't worry, youngster. Creatures come here, get healed, and then go back to the wild."

"Go back? You mean, they aren't going to hold us here?"

Bobby shook his head. "This isn't a prison. Once you're healthy, out you go."

"What about you?" Seven asked the cat boldly.

"I like it here. I can leave anytime. But they need someone to keep the nervous critters reassured."

As the cat spoke, Arnica crept to the edge of the examination table. "I like you," she said to the bobcat. "Your tail is like mine."

Seven caught her breath. Surely the bobcat wouldn't stand for such an insult.

To her surprise, he sat down and smiled. "Why, thank you. I think you have an especially nice tail."

"Big fish bit it off," explained Arnica.

"That must have hurt."

Arnica nodded. The bobcat stretched his head forward and touched her nose with his, a sign of affection.

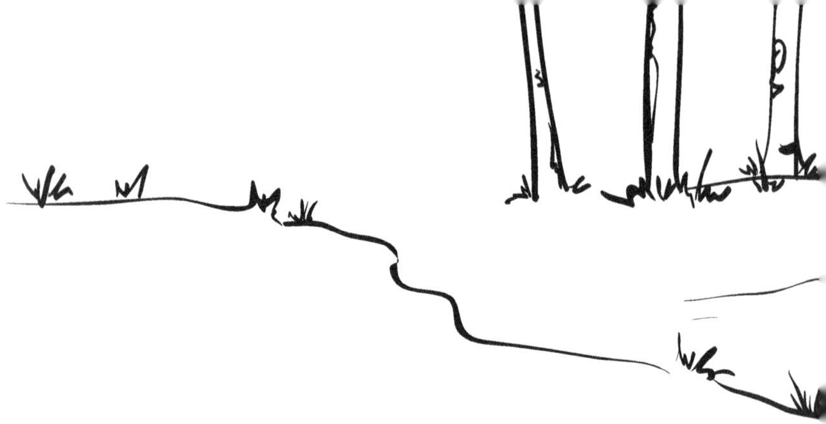

Chapter 15

At the clinic, the sisters slept in separate cages, but they were allowed to roam around during most of the day. This privilege was entirely due to Arnica's amiability. Faye and Colin seemed to believe that she would make sure that Seven behaved herself.

After only a few days, Arnica acted as if she owned the place. Besides riding on Colin's and Faye's shoulders, she tagged along behind the bobcat, eating from his bowl and curling up in his nest, a large dog bed in the clinic office. Bobby indulged Arnica's every request, and his affection extended to Seven—to her surprise. "I've never had kittens of my own," he explained to Seven as Arnica crawled all over him. "And I've seen a lot of creatures come and go, including a lot of raccoons. But you two are special." He paused to lick Arnica's face clean, and Arnica's eyes crossed with contentment.

"We'll be leaving soon," Seven said softly.

The bobcat raised his head. "How do you know?"

Seven sat up and scratched herself, although she wasn't itchy. "It's been days since the people last gave me that bitter drink," she said. "My bite is healed, the fur grown back. When the man weighed me today, he made a funny noise, like I had grown a lot. I feel strong and healthy. There's only one reason for me to stay."

Then they both looked at Arnica. Arnica had grown much less than Seven had. She was about half the size of her sister. Her stubby tail made climbing difficult, and when she did climb, she moved slowly. Faye and Colin had already had several whispered discussions about whether they should release her, fearing that if they did, she would die in the wild.

The cat spoke slowly, weighing each word. "You must think about what is best for her. If you asked her, she would go to the ends of the earth for you, because she loves you that much. Should she make the trip? That's another question entirely."

"But I promised I would take care of her," Seven said.

The cat said kindly, "She could not have a better home. I will watch over her myself. I promise you. Besides," he added, "a raccoon with seven rings has great things to accomplish."

"What? How?" Seven spluttered.

Bobby narrowed his eyes with amusement. "Don't look so surprised. I know the lore of the woods. My mother taught me the stories."

The clinic door banged open suddenly and made Seven jump. Human grunts rose above animal snarls and the sounds of a strong body flailing back and forth.

"What's going on?" Seven asked, scampering to the door.

A man in brown held a long pole with a lasso on the end, which was wrapped around the neck of a snarling coyote—the same coyote from Isabelle's house. The coyote spied Seven out of the corner of his eye and twisted his head to get a better look.

"You!" he snarled. He tried to lunge for her, but the pole held him firmly.

"Get the medetomidine!" Faye called.

Colin hurried over with a needle. As the coyote twisted and cursed at his captors, Colin stuck the needle into the angry animal's hind leg. After a few more curses, he settled down, eyelids drooping until they shut. The coyote sagged to the floor.

Seven ran back to Bobby. "A needle! They killed him!"

Bobby shook his head. "Sometimes needles kill. That one was meant to calm him down. Thrashing around so much, he could hurt himself worse."

Bobby and Seven went back to watch. Arnica snuggled down into Bobby's nest.

Colin and Faye placed the coyote onto the examination table. They X-rayed the coyote's leg and put a cast on it. Bobby explained that the plaster casts were used on animals that had broken legs, and broken legs often came from cars. "He's one of the lucky ones," Bobby said. "Animals don't usually survive getting hit by cars."

As they watched, the coyote bared his teeth in his sleep. Bobby observed, "You've made a powerful enemy, Seven-Rings Moon."

When the coyote awoke, Bobby told Seven and Arnica to stay in the office. As they watched, he sauntered out to the coyote's cage. "Evening, friend," the bobcat said, lying down on the floor.

The coyote shook his head to clear it. "Where am I?"

"You're in a wildlife clinic."

The coyote sniffed at the cast and sneezed. As if the sneeze had caused a connection to form in his mind, he demanded, "Where is the raccoon?"

Bobby said mildly, "We have several raccoons here."

The coyote snarled, "You know the one I mean, cat. She was in the doorway."

"Why are you so interested in that raccoon?"

"She tried to destroy me."

"I heard that you walked by an open door, and the dog jumped you. The raccoon just happened to be outside."

"No!" snarled the coyote. "She planned the whole thing. There is no way the big dog could have escaped without her help. I will find her, and I will kill her."

The cat stood up and stretched with a show of nonchalance that he didn't actually feel. "Suit yourself," he said. "Revenge is going to have to wait a while." He padded back to the office to where Seven anxiously waited by a dozing Arni.

Bobby said, "He is very angry. You both may be in danger."

Seven shook her head. "He never saw Arnica. He doesn't know that she exists. Please, Bobby, help me keep it that way."

He nodded. "We've had coyotes here before. Faye and Colin keep them under close observation. Tomorrow he'll probably be moved to one of the outdoor runs. That way he can move around more."

The bobcat was right. The next day, Colin and Faye moved the coyote outside. Seven squeezed against the back wall of her cage while Bobby lay on his dog bed, hiding Arnica under his massive paws. When they heard the chain-link door clang, both Bobby and Seven relaxed. Arnica pushed her way out from under the bobcat and sneezed. "What was that for?" she demanded as they walked into the cage area.

"We couldn't let the coyote see you," Bobby explained.

"You didn't have to sit on me," Arnica complained.

Faye came into the room. "There now, our irritable guest is safely outside. Now we can let you out for a little while to play with your friend." She unlatched Seven's cage. As the sisters touched noses, the woman sighed. "She sure will miss you," she said to Seven.

Seven-Rings's stomach tightened with dread. Perhaps the decision about whether to bring Arnica along on the journey to the Notch would not be hers to make.

One more week went by, a week that saw the departure of several animals and the arrival of an injured cottontail. Faye and Colin examined Arnica repeatedly and finally reached a decision.

Early the next morning, they brought three pet carriers into the clinic. Into the first two went two gray squirrels. The third was meant for Seven-Rings.

Faye took her gently from the cage. "Why don't you take a few minutes to say good-bye?" she said to Seven, placing her on the floor. Seven ran for the office, calling,

"Bobby! I need to talk to Arnica."

The cat led the way to his nest. Seven tumbled in beside her little sister. Arnica blinked and said, "Seven? What's wrong?"

"Arni, I have to go."

"Go where?"

"I'm going north—to the Notch."

"OK," said Arnica, standing up and stretching. "Me, too."

"Arni," Seven took a deep breath, then plunged ahead. "I want you to stay here."

"Stay?" The tiny raccoon looked confused.

"I know we were going to go to the Notch together. But I don't know what's going to happen. You will be safer here—with Bobby."

"You want me to stay here, with Bobby? And not go with you?"

Seven caught her sister's paw. "Stay here and keep an eye on him for me, will you? He needs you."

A shadow fell across them, and all three animals looked up to see Colin. "Come on, little one. It's time to go."

Seven pressed her forehead against Arnica's. Then Colin's hands caught her up and carried her back to the clinic. Arnica scrambled onto Bobby's back and they hurried to follow. Colin slid Seven into a carrier; limp with sadness, she didn't resist. The man carried her out to the pickup truck. Through the slits in the carrier's walls, Seven could just make out the faces of her little sister and her feline friend in the clinic's window, watching her as Colin's truck pulled away.

Chapter 16

The trip in the truck seemed to take forever. Seven listened dully as the squirrels chattered away in their excitement.

"Gonna be trees!" said one.

"Big trees!" said the other.

"Gonna be nuts!" said the first.

"Lots of nuts!" said the second.

On and on they went, chattering about leaves and grass and flowers and all the other things they imagined would be waiting for them at the release site. Seven didn't care. All she knew was one thing: Arnica wasn't with her anymore.

Colin parked the truck on a dirt road and took the squirrels out of the back. The squirrels bounced and boinged around their carriers, requiring him to grip the handles tightly.

"All right, all right!" the man said with feigned

exasperation. "I'll let you two fuzzy bouncy balls out of there." He placed both carriers on the ground and opened the doors.

Suddenly realizing that they were free, the squirrels hunkered down, gray balls of fur with huge, frightened eyes. Colin chuckled. "It's different when there's nothing between you and the big wide world, eh?" he asked.

He returned to the truck and got Seven's carrier. He placed it on the ground and unlatched the door. "Come on, sweetheart. Show them how it's done."

Seven poked her nose out of the carrier. The air smelled earthy, yet bright. Somewhere in the branches overhead, two blue jays were arguing over babysitting duties. Seven stepped out onto the cool grass and looked up at the man.

"Go ahead. You're all better. Good luck to you."

Seven sniffed and learned that deer, fox, and woodchucks had passed by. She turned left and began walking north. Her path took her past the huddled squirrels.

"There goes ra'coon!" said one.

"Ra'coon!" echoed the other.

"Maybe we should follow?" said the first.

"Yes! Follow!" said the second. And they scampered through the leaf litter behind her, next to her, and in front of her—apparently simultaneously.

"Whereyoo gonna go?" one squirrel asked her.

"Whatchoo gonna do?" the other chimed in.

They moved so fast and looked so much alike that Seven could not keep them straight. She did not want to. She wanted them to leave her alone. She sped up.

So did the squirrels.

She broke into a run.

So did the squirrels.

"We gonna run!" said one.

"Love to run!" said the other.

Anger and grief fueling her strides, Seven ran as fast as she could. Suddenly, the ground disappeared from under her paws, and she tumbled down an embankment.

"Whee!" screamed one squirrel.

"Rolly rolly!" shrieked the other.

Seven landed at the bottom of the embankment with a thud, and the two squirrels smacked into her. "Oof!" she grunted.

The squirrels leaped up. "Fun!" one said.

"Fun! Again!" cried the other.

Seven rose to her paws. "Stop it!" she snarled.

The squirrels paused.

"Leave me alone!" Seven hissed. "I am traveling

north—alone!"

"Alone, alone," said one squirrel.

"That doesn't sound fun," said the other.

"It's not, but that's the way it is," Seven said. She roughly brushed her paw across her mask.

Seeing this, one squirrel said, "You're sad. We're sorry. We didn't know."

"Didn't know," said the other, looking concerned.

"Well, there's nothing you can do about it," Seven-Rings said.

"Oh, yes!" exclaimed the first squirrel.

"Gonna do something!" said the second squirrel.

As one, they dashed into a patch of greenery and emerged carrying small dark-purple flowers in their mouths. They reached Seven and said, "Here." They held out the violets to her. "These violets are good to eat."

The flowers were delicious, and the squirrels' kindness soothed Seven's sadness.

The squirrels dialed down their jumping and bouncing a little, although not completely. One would dash partway up a tree trunk and then execute an expert backflip, nearly landing on the other. Not to be outdone, the second squirrel would race around the tree trunk, his sharp claws giving him perfect leverage on the bark.

Seven asked them their names. The backflip expert was Buckeye; the echo, Chokecherry. As she observed them,

Seven began to notice their subtle differences. Buckeye had more brown fur around his nose, while Chokecherry's tail was a bit longer. The easiest way to tell them apart, though, was through their speech. Buckeye always spoke first. He was older, he explained, and that was the squirrel way.

"Older talks first, and younger listens, adds to," Buckeye said.

"Add good stuff!" said Chokecherry.

"Hmm," mused Seven-Rings. "Sometimes I wonder if you just add a word to what Buckeye says so you can talk, too, Chokecherry."

"Add *good* stuff!" the squirrel repeated, insistent that even an adverb or adjective was a valuable addition to any conversation.

Seven-Rings opened her mouth to speak, but noticed that her companions had frozen in their tracks. She paused, and the smell came to her, too, drifting on the wind like smoke. She did not recognize it, but her instincts said to her, "Run, run, run!"

"What is it?" she asked Buckeye.

"Tree-tearer," the squirrel answered, his eyes wide.

"Tree-tearer? What . . .?"

Seven got her answer when a bear appeared out of the brush.

Chapter 17

The creature was a young male, with bright eyes, a sensitive nose, and very sharp claws.

"Wonderful! Appetizers!" he said, looking at Buckeye and Chokecherry. Before the bear finished speaking, the two squirrels shot up a nearby tree.

"Aw," the bear said. "Guess they'll be dessert instead."

Seven searched her mind for anything she knew about bears. Her mother, being a city raccoon, had never mentioned them, and none of the stories Runner had told about First Raccoon had mentioned bears. All she knew was what Bobby had said during an evening conversation about animals that rarely appeared at the clinic: Bears slept during the winter and ate mostly plants.

The bear growled, "Too bad for you, raccoon. My mother always said that raccoons are no-good bits of dirt—scavengers and thieves."

The insult made Seven-Rings' hackles rise. "Better a scavenger than a slugabed," she retorted.

From far overhead, Buckeye called, "Why you annoy bear?"

Chokecherry added, "Big bear!"

"Because he's a bully," Seven shot back. "And I don't like bullies."

The bear looked hurt. "What do you mean, I'm a bully?" Then he rose onto his hind legs and roared, "I'm the biggest creature in these woods! I can do whatever I want! And that includes eating you!"

He fell to all fours and lunged forward. Seven-Rings leaped backward, swung her left paw, and scratched the bear's nose. Roaring with pain, the bear shook his head. As the bear lunged again, Seven spun around and raced away. The bear pounded along behind. Above, Buckeye and Chokecherry ran through the branches, following the pursuit.

"What am I doing?" Seven-Rings thought. Ahead, she heard the rushing of a river. She turned right and tried to run faster. The bear snapped at her tail as she suddenly changed direction. She heard him skid and hit a tree with a loud crash. His mishap bought her a few seconds to reach the water's edge. She crawled out onto a fallen log and turned to face the bear.

His sides were heaving. "You think you're pretty clever, don't you?" he snarled. "You're not so smart now."

Seven backed out further on the fallen tree. Below her, the water foamed as it hurtled past.

"What's the matter, raccoon? No sassy remarks? No snappy comebacks?" The bear stepped on the fallen log. It shuddered under his weight.

"One . . ." said Seven.

"Say what you want, it's going to end the same," the bear said. He stepped up onto the log, which rocked slightly under his weight.

"Two," said Seven.

"What?" The bear scowled. "You're not making any sense. So, raccoons are not only deadbeats, but idiots as well?"

"Three!" cried Seven. She launched herself into the air. Startled, the bear stumbled backward. The raccoon bounded off his head and his back and scampered to the bank.

Snarling, the bear tried to spin around, but the sudden movement made the log shift under his feet. The bear landed with a huge splash in the river. The current caught him and swept him downstream, roaring with anger.

The squirrel brothers skittered down to the ground and leaped around Seven-Rings. "You're smart!" exclaimed Buckeye.

"Very, very smart!" added Chokecherry.

Seven shrugged. "He was just too big for the log."

The squirrels looked at each other knowingly. "And modest," said Buckeye. "That's why you never talked about who you were when we were at the clinic."

"But we knew right away," said Chokecherry. "We counted the rings. We knew you were the raccoon born when the moon turned copper. And we knew what you're going to do. We knew the old climbing song!"

Together, the squirrel brothers recited, "When to you life trouble brings/find a raccoon with seven rings/born beneath a copper moon/then all your problems will end soon." Buckeye added proudly, "First Squirrel made that up."

Seven started walking, and the squirrels bounced along next to her. "So you squirrels think I'm special, too? How do you know I'm the right raccoon?"

"It is the Forest Story," explained Chokecherry, for once not repeating what his brother had said. "All of us know the story—that's why the bobcat could tell you were special, and we knew right away that you were meant for big things. Not only will you see the Notch, you'll save it!"

"And we'll get to see you do it!" said Buckeye. He turned to his brother, a look of delight on his face. "And the squirrels will make up climbing songs about us!"

Seven-Rings continued her journey north, her two cheerful companions bouncing along beside her and making up terrible rhymes.

CHAPTER 18

The story of the bear's dunking spread quickly through the woods. The birds, who love a good story, told the tale to any creature who would listen. Some accounts were more factual than others, depending on whether the teller was a matter-of-fact wren or a more inventive bluebird. Within hours, Seven-Rings found herself the object of admiration wherever she walked. Buckeye and Chokecherry became her honor guard. Even the large animals—the deer and the moose—stared at her.

"So, you're the famous bear-beating raccoon, are you?" asked a masked stranger who appeared in their path. He was a little older and a shade bigger than Seven-Rings. His eyes twinkled as he spoke.

She stopped and sat up. "And who wants to know?" she asked. Buckeye and Chokecherry took to the trees, the

better to watch and listen.

"My name's Waxwing," he answered.

"Waxwing? Isn't that a bird?"

He shrugged. "My mum is crazy about birds. Named us all after the feathered beasties." An angry chitter from above indicated that some bird had taken offense at being called a beastie. "Yep, in my litter there was me, my brother Cardinal, my sister Viero, and my other sister Sparrow. So tell me, did you really push a bear into the river?" he asked.

Despite herself, Seven-Rings found the stranger charming, and so she told him the real story. He listened closely, ears flicking at certain points. "There wasn't really any need for that bluebird to embellish," he said. "The real story is exciting enough."

"I didn't mean for it to be," Seven-Rings admitted. "I just wasn't in the mood to be pushed around. I was lucky."

"I don't think it was all luck," Waxwing said.

"Well, you can think what you like. I've got to get going." She dropped to all fours and resumed walking, going around him to stay on the trail.

Waxwing followed, saying, "You know, there aren't that many raccoons in these woods. Not since the Madness came through. Killed us off by the dozens."

His words formed a memory in Seven's mind: Fig had said something about a sickness. "What is the Madness?" she asked Waxwing.

He shuddered. "It's horrible. You're dying of thirst but terrified of water. You're so angry, you'll pick a fight with anything from the light of the moon to the leaves on the trees. And finally, you die." As he spoke, his voice filled with pain.

Seven-Rings paused. "You—you saw someone die this way, didn't you?"

He nodded. "We had never had the sickness here. Then

three sick ones came. The people brought them."

"Which people?"

"Does it matter?"

Thinking of the people at the rehab center, she said, "It does. It's very important."

"I didn't see them, but my brother did. He saw a group of men in hunting clothes. They had caught the sick ones somewhere else and brought them here." He paused for a moment. "But the mad ones found us. They found the foxes, too. That's why all the foxes are gone from here. That's what my mother told us. She told us to always remember. And always be on guard."

Softly, he said, "If it weren't for my mother, we all would have died."

Seven listened closely. Something about the story tickled the back of her mind. She began walking again, but she was so busy chasing the memory that she did not notice that Waxwing had fallen in by her side.

It had been the bats. Early one morning, Runner had taken Seven with her to await the return of the colony's leader from a night of hunting. One of the oldest bats in the colony had crept over to sit with them. The old female bat could no longer fly, but her mind was still bright and sharp. Seven had listened, fascinated, as the old bat told of the colony where she had grown up. "I was one of the few who lived through our first summer," the old bat had said.

"My mother knew that some of the bats in our colony had a disease. They were not sick enough to die, but they made the newborn bats sick."

Seven shuddered as she remembered the look in the bat's eyes as she explained what happened. "Little ones could not fight the disease. Almost all that year's newborns died. My mother hid me away in a crack in the wall, guarding me with her own body, refusing to allow any others near, not even my father. Finally, we left; I held her fur tightly as she flew night after night. We found this place, where there was no sickness. You call it the Madness; we call it Fly-No-More. Humans call it rabies." The conversation had ended then, as the rest of the colony returned.

Seven realized that Waxwing was walking next to her, and that the squirrel brothers had disappeared. As if casting off a shadow, Waxwing said cheerfully, "Well, we're here, right? And I've met a remarkable raccoon today—who still hasn't told me where she is going."

Reluctant to reveal too much, yet finding Waxwing appealing, Seven said, "I'm going north."

"That's a big place, north."

She took a deep breath and said, "I'm going to the Notch."

Waxwing said, "OK."

"That's all you have to say?"

He looked at her in surprise. "I don't have anything else to say because I don't know what the Notch is."

She paused. "The Notch is the home of the raccoons."

"Oh," he said. They walked for a moment in awkward silence. Then Waxwing said, "There are lots of raccoons around here. Maybe here is what you're looking for."

At that, dozens of raccoons appeared out of the undergrowth and encircled Seven-Rings and Waxwing. The circle parted, and a large female swaggered up to them. Waxwing said, "This is my mum, Sprucewood. She's in charge around here."

Although not nearly as large as Greyson had been, the female was imposing nonetheless. She sat up and studied Seven-Rings. "You came from the rescue place, didn't you, dearie?" she said, her voice surprisingly high-pitched.

"How did you know?"

Sprucewood said, "The birds aren't the only ones with eyes in this forest. We've been watching you since you arrived. We keep a close eye on new arrivals, ever since the Madness," the female said. "We need to make sure that they aren't carriers."

"That explains how you helped me with the bear," Seven said sarcastically.

Ignoring the remark, Sprucewood said, "Why don't you join us for dinner? Meet the rest of the family?"

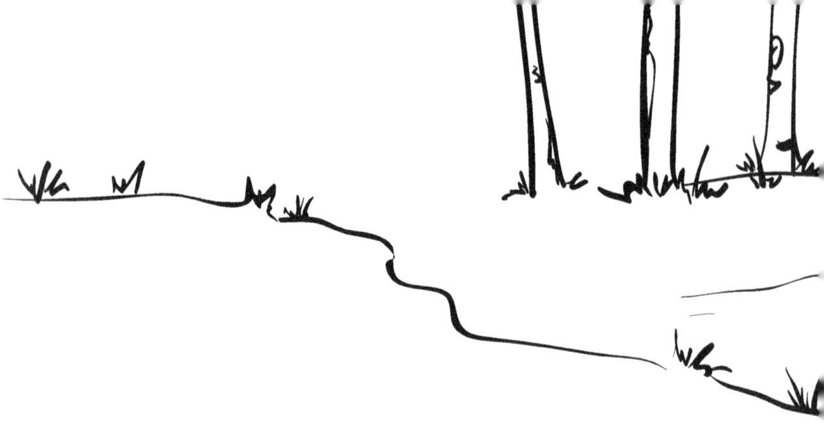

Chapter 19

Uneasily, but with Waxwing by her side, Seven followed the rest of the raccoons across a meadow and into a stand of pines. The branches of five trees intertwined, forming a roof of sorts over a soft layer of needles that was thick with age. Each paw step released a fragrant puff of pine scent. The softness felt luxurious under Seven's feet, like the cushions on the sofa back in the old church. Deep hollows in the needles showed where the raccoons slept. Many places were empty, but two were occupied by sleepy babies and their mothers. Seven guessed that at least thirty raccoons lived in that place.

"Welcome," said Sprucewood. "You're our honored guest, Bear-bane!" She clapped her paws, and, as if from nowhere, raccoons appeared, carrying roots, minnows, acorns, and berries. Seven noticed that no one, not even the youngest kit, sneaked a bite. She wondered how Typhoo would have handled the situation.

Then the family members arranged themselves around the food. "You're here, next to me," Sprucewood said to Seven. Waxwing stood on her other side. A grizzled male, whose name was Corm, took the place across from her. He looked at Seven, and sorrow flitted across his face.

"My family!" Sprucewood began. "We have come together to celebrate a remarkable event. This afternoon, our scouts witnessed a confrontation between a raccoon and the great stink beast." It took a moment for Seven-Rings to realize Sprucewood was talking about the bear. "The result of this confrontation reaffirms the natural superiority of raccoons to all other forest creatures. It is with great pride I present Seven-Rings!"

The assembled raccoons cheered, but the weakness of the sound made Seven think that they were cheering because it was expected rather than because they wanted to. "Thank you, but I was just—," she began, and then caught a tiny head shake from Corm. She changed what she had been about to say—that escaping the bear had been largely luck—and concluded, "I was just so delighted to be invited to meet you."

Sprucewood looked pleased at Seven's words. At her signal, everyone turned their attention to the food. No one spoke as they ate.

As Waxwing handed her another minnow, Seven noticed that the fish, eggs, and blueberries were closest to Sprucewood. Raccoons that were seated a bit further away were eating blackberries and acorns. The most distant raccoons were making the best of a meager meal of roots, leaves, and pine seeds. Seven looked at the minnow in her paws and put it back. The movement caught Sprucewood's eye. "Something wrong?" she said.

"No, no. I'm just full," Seven-Rings lied.

With a sideways glance at Seven, Sprucewood snatched up the fish before anyone else could reach it. Waxwing and Corm did not look up.

After the food was gone, Sprucewood turned to Seven. "Now, as our guest, you will favor us with a story," the older female said.

A story! She wracked her brain, searching for a story that would not make her host upset with her. Of course! A story about the First Raccoon would please everyone. Seven cleared her throat and began.

"In the days of First Raccoon, the animals decided to play a ball game. On one side was Hawk, Turkey, and Jay. On the other side was Skunk, Fox, and Mouse. Although Skunk, Fox, and Mouse tried very hard, they could not stop the birds from flying upward with the ball and dropping it into their goal. They could not score, because the birds dove at them repeatedly.

"First Raccoon was among the spectators. She frowned as the score grew more and more lopsided. Hawk, Turkey, and Jay began to taunt their opponents for playing so poorly—especially First Mouse, who was trying very hard, but couldn't keep up because of his very short legs.

"At last, halftime came. While First Fox and First Skunk got water, First Raccoon took First Mouse aside. 'I have an idea,' she said.

"First Raccoon led First Mouse to the red oak tree. She removed several leaves and fastened them to First Mouse's tiny legs. 'Flap the leaves hard,' First Raccoon said. First Mouse did. Suddenly he was flying!

"When play resumed, First Mouse scored over and over again, and he stole the ball from the birds in midair. At the end of the game, the score was tied. Hawk, Turkey, and Jay complained bitterly that First Mouse had cheated. 'I am no longer just a mouse,' First Mouse declared, flapping his wings. 'To celebrate, I am taking a new name. I am now First Bat.'

"While the others cheered, Hawk, Turkey, and Jay went off in a huff. To this day, they will not share the sky with bats, who fly only at night and always greet raccoons politely."

When she finished, she was pleased with herself, but her audience was silent, looking at Sprucewood for clues as to how they should react.

After an agonizing moment, Sprucewood said. "Good story. But it would have been better if you had told it properly."

Seven was stunned. She'd heard the story dozens of times. She opened her mouth to speak but felt Waxwing's paw grip her foreleg in warning.

Sprucewood stood up, shook herself, and declared that it was bedtime. The raccoons walked quietly to the depressions in the pine needles. They curled up, hiding their faces within their bushy tails. A couple of kits struggled against their mothers' grips, but the females restrained their youngsters, watching Sprucewood with unease as they quieted their babies. Held tightly, the kits eventually stopped struggling and fell asleep.

In the depression she had been assigned, Seven lay as still as possible, but her eyes and ears moved constantly. She listened to the soft steps of the guards and patrols as they moved in and out of the grove. Sprucewood slumbered peacefully, but neither Waxwing nor Corm were fully asleep. Except for Sprucewood, no one seemed to be enjoying a good night's rest.

At last, her tension got the better of her. Walking as softly as she could, she made her way to the edge of the grove.

A large female raccoon appeared in her path. "Where are you going?"

"I, er . . ." she fumbled.

Suddenly Corm was standing next to her. "It's all right, Thistle," he said. "No one remembered to show our guest the latrine."

Thistle stood aside and let them pass. They walked for a way in silence, until Corm looked behind them. "It is all right," he said. "We can speak freely here. My mate's spies have some sense of decorum, at least."

"Spies? What do you mean?"

His face was full of sorrow. "My mate has gone mad with power. We are no family. We are slaves who must worship where she walks and what she does."

Suddenly Seven realized what had been wrong with her story. "My tale—it should have been about Sprucewood, shouldn't it?"

Corm nodded. "As silly as it sounds, all stories told here feature our leader. In her eyes, she is First Raccoon."

Seven covered her mouth with a paw. After a moment, she said, "Why don't you stop her?"

"I cannot," Corm said sadly. "If I were to try, she would kill the only living thing I love: our son, Waxwing. He is the only child I have left."

He glanced back toward the sleeping area. "Sprucewood was not always this way. But then came the Madness. It infected the leaders of our clan. Sprucewood drove them away. She was very brave. But what she did went to her head. She assumed the role of leader without a vote. She killed anyone who opposed her—including our own kits."

Seven longed to comfort the old raccoon, but she did not dare. Instead, she asked, "Does Waxwing know what happened to his brother and sisters?"

"No!" Corm's voice rose with alarm, then fell to an urgent whisper. "He mustn't find out. He thinks they have gone exploring in the wide world. I know the truth. And now, you do, too."

Softly, Seven-Rings said, "Why are you telling me this?"

"I know the prophecy. A raccoon with seven black rings on her tail will solve all our problems."

Seven recalled, uneasily, the squirrel song that Buckeye and Chokecherry had sung for her, and how they believed that she would make all their problems go away. Corm paused and cocked an ear, listening to the sounds of the night. "You must be careful, because Sprucewood knows the prophecy as well. Come, we must return. We'll be missed if we are gone too long."

Chapter 20

Seven was relieved to see the sun rise, but did not know what the day would hold. Corm acted as though nothing had happened. Waxwing was eager to share breakfast with her, running over as soon as she appeared near the food area. "Good morning!" he said cheerfully. "Did you sleep well?"

"Yes, thanks," she said, accepting the acorn he offered. She made quick work of it, and dropped the cap and shell at her feet. Waxwing quickly scoooped them up.

Sprucewood appeared. A silence fell over the raccoons. She ignored them all and walked straight to Seven-Rings.

"Did you sleep well?" she asked, eyes glittering.

Instantly on her guard, Seven nodded.

"Excellent," said Sprucewood. "We will spend the day together. Where is my food?" This last part was said with a snarl, and a small raccoon that reminded Seven of her sister scurried up. He looked frightened.

"There is a problem, Sprucewood," the little raccoon squeaked.

The big female glared at him. "What kind of a problem?"

"The acorn stores have been raided," said the little raccoon.

"What?"

"I don't know what happened," said the little raccoon. "The guards were stationed as normal."

Sprucewood lunged for the little raccoon, bowling him over and snapping at his face and forepaws. "I'll—show—you—what's—normal!" she snarled.

Seven watched in horror as the little raccoon shrieked under the assault. She stared at the rest of the raccoons, all of whom—even Waxwing and Corm—were looking at the ground. She opened her mouth to shout "Stop!" when a voice behind her called, "Sprucewood!"

The leader broke off her attack and spun to face the newcomer. It was the female raccoon, Thistle. A larger male was behind her, and they were each gripping a struggling squirrel.

"Let go!" cried a familiar voice.

"Yes, let go quickly!" added the next voice.

Thistle said, "We found them raiding the acorn stores."

"We were not raiding! There was enough there for everyone! We took just five acorns!" Buckeye said.

"Five each!" Chokecherry added.

His brother glared at him. "Not helping!"

"No one steals food from the Sprucewood Clan and gets away with it," said Sprucewood. "Kill them!"

"No!" Seven-Rings exclaimed. "These two squirrels are my friends. They didn't mean any harm."

Sprucewood looked at her through narrowed eyes. "You are calling these lesser creatures your friends?"

"They're not lesser creatures. They are Buckeye and Chokecherry. We are traveling together. Yes, we're friends."

Sprucewood sat back on her haunches. "That is not acceptable. Raccoons do not associate with the likes of these."

Seven bristled. "I don't care what you think is acceptable. I won't stand by and see my friends harmed." She heard one of the raccoons gasp.

Sprucewood's eyes glittered. "Very well. We'll make an example of you, too."

A sudden squeal of pain came from Thistle. Chokecherry had sunk his teeth into the raccoon's foreleg. Buckeye did the same, and the two squirrels scampered free of their captors. As the squirrels shot up a tree, Seven bolted.

She soon realized that she could not outrun Sprucewood's family. There were too many, and they knew their territory too well. It would be just a matter of time before they trapped her. She blundered up a shrub and shouted, "Buckeye!"

The squirrel appeared at her shoulder instantly.

"I can't outrun them," Seven panted. "I need to find a river or something."

"Right," Buckeye replied, and zipped to the top of the towering shrub. He was back in a moment. "Northwest! I think it's a river."

Seven slid backwards down the branches of the shrub and hit the ground running. A few minutes later, she found not water, but pavement. Buckeye's river was actually a road.

The clatter of leaves and twigs behind her signaled the arrival of the other raccoons. Sprucewood was at their head. "Now you will die!"

Seven jumped backward. Sprucewood sprang after her. She sunk her teeth into Seven's ear. Seven shrieked with pain. She twisted her body to escape. Her ear tore.

"I know what you've done, Sprucewood," Seven gasped, despite the explosion of pain in her ear. "You saved your people, but made them slaves."

Sprucewood snorted. "Someone needs to lead." She snapped at Seven's right foreleg, but the younger raccoon leaped upward, and Sprucewood's teeth clapped shut on empty air. Sprucewood howled, "There will be no prophecy fulfilled here!" She leaped at Seven-Rings, and they rolled over and over into the road.

Suddenly a terrible roar shook both their bodies. Seven tore herself loose from Sprucewood's grip and dove for the side of the road. A blast of wind rolled her head-over-tail and threw dirt into her eyes. A truck roared past, horn blaring. Then, as suddenly as it had come, it was gone.

Sprucewood lay unmoving in the middle of the road. Corm and Waxwing crept over to her. Corm sat up and shook his head. Waxwing made his way to Seven-Rings. "Are you all right?"

"I'll survive," she said. "She didn't have the sickness, did she?"

"No. Not the one we all fear so much. But we should have paid more attention to the signs that she was not right," he said. He began to lick Seven's wounds.

The others, including Corm, gathered around them. "What will we do now?" asked Waxwing.

"Now, we take care of each other," said Corm. "We will live as raccoons are supposed to. We will share equally. We will be part of the forest, not apart from it. We will be better than before." He turned to Seven. "You really are welcome to stay, if you like."

She shook her head. "I think it's best that I go," she said. "I've caused you so much grief."

"On the contrary," said Waxwing. "You've saved our lives."

At Corm's surprised squeak, Waxwing said, "Don't look so surprised, Father. I knew what was going on. I found Sparrow." His voice broke. "I knew what had happened to her, and who had done it. Thank you for protecting me. For protecting all of us."

A murmur ran through the assembled raccoons. Corm said, "We will be all right. We will return to the pine grove. We will bury your mother with honor. Despite the wrongs she did, she did protect us from the sickness. She should be honored for that."

Solemnly, Corm and Waxwing lifted the body of Sprucewood from where it lay on the roadway. With a nod to Seven, they led the way back into the woods.

Buckeye and Chokecherry emerged from the trees, took Seven's forelegs, and gently led her away in the opposite direction.

Chapter 21

On the north side of the road, the land rose steeply, and in her exhausted state, Seven found the climb especially difficult. Halfway to the summit, Buckeye found an empty burrow between two rocks. She crawled in. The squirrel brothers took turns watching over her as she slept. When she emerged two days later, the sky was gray and the day drizzly, but she tackled the rest of the high hill without difficulty.

Before her lay a sight she had never imagined. At the foot of the hill lay a town, and beyond the town rose mountains, their tops lost in mist. Perhaps, she thought, the Notch was hidden among them somewhere.

Because it was early, the town was not yet fully awake. Early risers were preparing their shops for tourists and bargain hunters. Many of the visitors arrived in the downtown area for breakfast, but the smells of cooking bacon and pancakes held no charm for Seven at the moment. Instead, she crept under a shrub and watched the people come and go, while the squirrels went off to find their breakfast. She dozed for a couple of hours, until the squirrels returned with several acorns, which she ate gratefully.

Seven and her friends continued to the far edge of a park, which ended at a sidewalk and a street. Cars, trucks, and all manner of vehicles zoomed past. "How are we going to get across?" asked Buckeye, his eyes wide as he watched the speeding traffic.

A movement up above caught Seven's eye. A crow had landed on a strip of wire overhead. "Brangwy!" shouted Seven.

"This way!" called the crow. Seven realized that the wire ran between two tall, naked trees—one on each side of the street. "Come on, guys! I've got a way!"

When the sidewalk was clear, she darted over to the naked tree and began to climb quickly. The squirrels caught on and beat her to the top, which had thick, square branches that were easy to sit on. Seven could feel a strange vibration with her whiskers. "This is no ordinary tree," she said.

Brangwy, who had watched their approach with amusement, called, "Better watch out. You'll get zapped if not careful!"

"Zapped? What's that?"

"This is no tree. This is an electric pole. It can zap you," said the crow. "Put all your feet on the wire at once. If you do, no zap."

"What do you think?" asked Buckeye. Chokecherry's tail flicked rapidly, showing his excitement at the challenge of the crossing.

"I trust her," replied Seven. "I'll go first." She tensed her muscles tightly, locked her eyes on the wire, and leaped. Her front paws caught, but her rear ones didn't. She found herself hanging from the wire.

From below, Seven heard a startled human cry. "Look!" exclaimed a woman. "That poor animal!"

"Somebody call 911!" yelled someone else.

Gritting her teeth, Seven pulled herself up. "Good job!" croaked Brangwy.

Being natural aeronauts, the squirrels made the leap without incident, and followed Seven across the wire. When they reached the far side, Brangwy said, "You've got an audience."

The bird was right. A crowd of people stood around the base of the pole, watching them curiously. The voices from the crowd drifted up to them. "Aren't they supposed to be hibernating?"

A woman in a white shirt and dark blue shorts rode up on a bicycle. "Did someone call 911?" she asked.

"I did, officer!" said a woman in a big hat. "Those

animals need help." She pointed up at Seven, Buckeye, and Chokecherry.

The police officer took off her sunglasses and looked up at the three animals huddled on the pole. She said dryly, "Looks to me like the only help those animals need is some space. They want to get down, but they're too scared because we're all standing here. If you want to help them, go on your way."

"But—," began the woman in the big hat.

The officer held up her hand. "Let's move along, folks, and give these critters some privacy and a chance to climb down."

Muttering, the watchers dispersed, clearly disappointed that the police officer wasn't going to climb the pole and rescue the poor stranded creatures. After they had moved away, the officer called up, "OK, you guys, you're on your own!" She got back on her bike and pedaled away.

Seven marveled at the power the woman had had over the other humans. Was it her white shirt? Her bicycle?

"That was close!" said Chokecherry as they scampered down the pole. Then Buckeye tackled him and they rolled about on the ground.

Brangwy swooped down. "Two things to know," she said. "First: a shadow follows you—sharp nose, sharper teeth, and moving fast. Better hurry because the shadow means to catch you!"

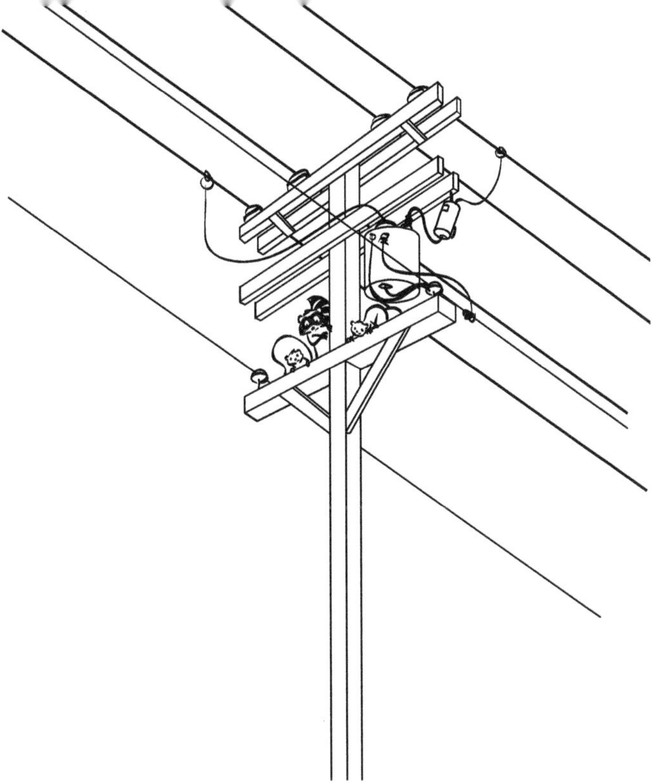

"A shadow?" asked Buckeye nervously.

"What shadow?" asked Chokecherry.

Seven's voice came out as a whisper. "The coyote."

It took a moment for the squirrels to remember. "From the healing place!" Buckeye squeaked.

"Very dangerous," Chokecherry observed. He added, "Very angry, too."

"Maybe we should split up," Seven said. "You don't need to stay with me. You're just putting yourselves at risk."

The squirrels conferred for a moment behind raised

tails, then they scampered ahead. "Come on," Buckeye teased. "We go!"

"We go!" said Chokecherry.

"Wait!" Seven said. "Brangwy, what's the second thing to know?"

The crow ruffled her feathers. "I heard things. About the Notch."

"I know. There's a road."

"Not just a road. Now the trees are being cut. My cousin says he heard that there is a plan to take all the ancient trees out of the Notch. There will be people, and buildings." She looked distressed. "You must hurry. There is not much time left."

Together, the raccoon and the squirrels continued down the alley, looking for the most direct route out of town. They crossed a wooden footbridge over a small river that rushed and tumbled on its way east. Ferns growing on the opposite side gave them cover until the sidewalk ended at a small forest. With squeals of delight, Buckeye and Chokecherry leaped from branch to branch, bouncing and springing. Brangwy soared overhead for a mile or so, and then vanished, as crows are apt to do.

They traveled until nightfall, when the rain began. Then, they found a tree that was developing a hollow and snuggled into it, Seven on the bottom, Buckeye and Chokecherry on the top. As the rain fell and the thunder crashed above, they curled up together. "Like home," said Buckeye.

"Like home, but I was always on the bottom," Chokecherry noted.

Seven suddenly realized that she knew little about the squirrel brothers. "How did you end up at the rescue center?"

"It's embarrassing," said Buckeye.

"Very embarrassing," agreed Chokecherry.

"What do you mean?" Seven said.

The squirrels shared a guilty look and then turned to face Seven. "We were foolish," Buckeye said. "We decided that living inside a house was easier than living outside in the trees."

Chokecherry took up the story. "Inside there was soft fluff to sleep in, and we could come and go."

"But then there was the wire," said Buckeye. Both squirrels shared a sorrowful look. "You see, there used to be three of us."

Buckeye continued. "It looked like a vine, but it wasn't. There were sparks, a fire. Our brother could not escape." At that, the squirrels fell silent, looking miserable at the memory of their loss.

"I'm sorry," Seven whispered.

Her friends snuggled against her. Sounding far older than his age, Buckeye said, "Faye and Colin healed our bodies. Time is healing our hearts."

At that, the conversation was over.

CHAPTER 22

A shaft of sunlight woke Seven. Chokecherry still dozed, but Buckeye was gone. "Where's Buckeye?" she asked the sleeping squirrel, nudging him until he opened his eyes.

Chokecherry looked around. "Dunno," he said sleepily. Together they climbed out of the hollow tree and perched on its edge. The air was fresh and still. Birds sang and quarreled and twittered. The smell of damp earth was intoxicating.

"There," said Chokecherry. He pointed to a maple tree a little ways off. A ripple ran through the branches, from the far side to the near. Two gray squirrels appeared.

"Morning, sleepies!" called Buckeye cheerily. The other squirrel didn't say anything until they all clustered around the hollow. "This is Elm. She lives here."

"Buckeye said you might be hungry," said Elm. "Come

with me. I know where there is good food." She turned and scurried down the trunk, heading for the ground.

Seven could tell that there were lots of good things in this patch of woods. Below her, she could hear the earthworms digging their tunnels and crunchy beetles scampering in the undergrowth. But Elm moved in a straight line, leading them unerringly toward an old tree stump, in which there was a stash of nuts and mushrooms.

As they ate, Seven watched Elm and Buckeye. They couldn't take their eyes off each other. This fascination was not lost on Chokecherry, who ate more and more slowly until he finally stopped eating altogether. Seven stretched out a hind paw and tapped him playfully. "You OK?" The usually cheerful squirrel cast his eyes down and shook his head. Seven's heart ached to see her friend so downcast.

Suddenly, more bouncing branches signaled the arrival of other squirrels. They tumbled out of the trees, jumping on and over Elm, swatting at each other, nipping playfully at each other's tails.

Seven, Buckeye, and Chokecherry stared.

"Stop! Stop!" Elm cried. "We have company!" After a moment, during which Elm got bopped on the head by one of the new arrivals, they lined up. Elm turned to Buckeye and said, "These are my sisters. I'm the oldest. Then there's Willow," she pointed to a squirrel who was getting her ear chewed on by another. "The ear-chewer is my youngest

sister, Juniper." Juniper waved. Seven liked her instantly. "Then there's Aspen," she said, pointing to the squirrel who was hanging on to her tail. "And last there's Maple."

Maple, it turned out, had eyes only for Chokecherry. Yet it was hard to say who was more shy.

The five female squirrels asked lots of questions, most of which Seven was content to let Buckeye and Chokecherry answer. She had practically tuned them out when one question caught her attention: "Is that the magic raccoon?"

Juniper said, "We've heard stories—from the birds."

Seven said, "Birds tend to exaggerate."

"But you did escape the truck, didn't you?" Juniper pressed.

"I was lucky."

Juniper jumped in front of Seven. "There's no such thing as luck. You stopped the houses. You crossed the big water. You soaked the bear!" Juniper insisted.

"I was never alone," Seven said. "I had lots of help from my friends. In fact, these fine gentlemen have been instrumental in my journey." Her statement distracted the others, making them turn their attention back to Buckeye and Chokecherry. But Juniper studied her closely. "You are magic," she said. "I saw your seven rings."

She turned to her sisters. "Remember the climbing song? This is the raccoon it's about! She's going to solve all our problems!" She spun back to Seven and said, "You're going to the Notch, aren't you? I'm coming with you."

"Oh, please," drawled Willow. "You always believed those old stories. They're just stories. There's no such place as the Notch. Mama just told you those stories to make you go to sleep."

"The Notch is real!" Juniper shot back.

Remembering her argument with the fox at the healing center, Seven said, "You're right, Juniper. The Notch is real. And I need to get there as soon as I can. It's in trouble." Seven sighed. "But I don't need any more traveling companions. These two are enough."

"Those two?" asked Juniper.

Seven turned. Buckeye was deep in earnest conversation with Elm. Chokecherry and Maple were looking at each other. Willow and Aspen looked on. Buckeye and Chokecherry were clearly torn, looking back and forth between Seven and the female squirrels.

Seven shook her head. "Don't worry about me. Colin and Faye made you better so you could live a normal life, not follow me."

Buckeye said, "But, you need us."

"Need us badly," echoed Chokecherry.

Seven smiled at her friends. "I need you to be happy. If you want to stay, then you should stay."

"But. . .," they began.

"I will be fine," she said, with a confidence she didn't really feel.

Touching noses with her, Buckeye said, "Be safe, Seven-Rings."

Chokecherry said, "I hope you find joy—and the

Notch, of course." With that, the squirrels vanished into the trees. Seven watched them go, and turned to Juniper. "Ready?"

In answer, Juniper leaped to the nearest trunk, scampered to the canopy, and began racing northward. Seven stayed on the ground but went as fast as she could. The day was clear and bright, and good for running. The wind in her whiskers made her feel very much alive, and, for the first time in a long while, happy.

She was surprised when she realized that Juniper had stopped and appeared to be looking behind them. She put her forefeet on the trunk and called, "What is it?"

As she waited for a reply, she grew aware of a distant thrumming, the sound of running feet pounding along the forest floor. Alarm shot through her. "Juniper! Is it a coyote?"

"No," the squirrel answered. "But . . ."

Seven didn't hear what Juniper said, because a furry form barreled into her and they tumbled end over end.

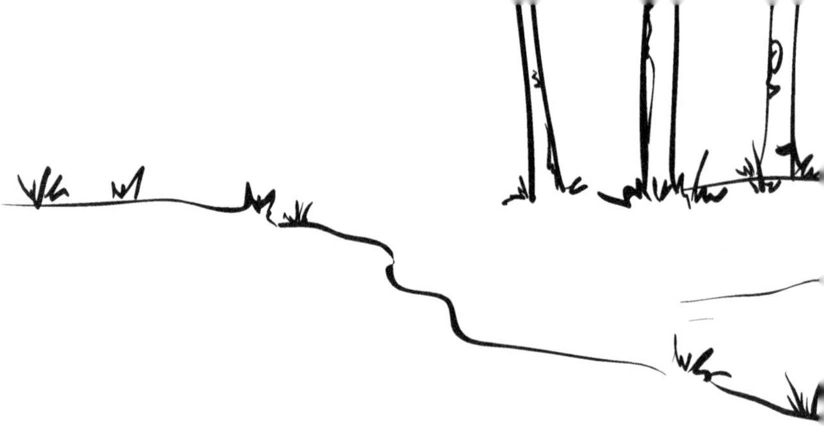

Chapter 23

"Waxwing!" she exclaimed.

Juniper leaped from the tree to stand beside Seven. "You know this—raccoon?" she asked.

Waxwing looked nothing like he had when she had last seen him. He was much thinner, and his coat looked dull. Plainly, he had eaten little and slept less.

"Thank First Raccoon!" Waxwing said. "I've found you! You're in danger!" He collapsed to the ground.

"Juniper! He needs water!"

"There's a spring nearby." Together, Seven and Juniper helped the exhausted raccoon to the spring. He sprawled on his back, breathing hard. Seven cupped her forepaws and dipped them into the cool water.

"There's no time!" he gasped.

"Shh. Drink."

Obediently, Waxwing lapped up the water, then lay back again. "More?"

"In a bit; if you drink too much or too fast you'll be sick," Seven said. "Juniper, keep watch." The squirrel nodded and disappeared.

Waxwing's breathing steadied. "I thought I'd never see you again," he said.

Seven said. "Why are you here?"

He began, "After Mum's death, Corm tried to get things back to normal for us—no more fear, no more special treatment for certain raccoons. He continued the regular patrols, because that seemed like a sensible thing to do. One full moon after you left, a raccoon on patrol encountered a coyote. He pounced on her before she could even greet him. 'Where is she?' he demanded. 'Who?' she asked. 'The raccoon that tricked me,' he answered. She didn't know what he was talking about, but she convinced him to follow her to the pine grove. Of course, Corm knew that the coyote was after you. He sent me north right away to look for you. He said he was going to send the coyote west as a diversion and buy me some time." He coughed, and Seven gave him another drink of water. "I ran as fast as I could. And I found you. You have to be careful."

"I heard about the coyote, Waxwing. A crow named Brangwy told me that he was behind me." Waxwing looked crestfallen that his news had already been received. "But

Brangwy found me by accident. I might never have known the real news without you."

He brightened slightly, despite his exhaustion. "What are you going to do?"

"I am going to the top of the mountain. I will wait for him there. Then I will go on to the Notch."

"How are you going to defeat him?"

"I have no idea."

Waxwing and Juniper insisted on accompanying her to the top of the mountain. Seven wished they would change their minds, but they would not be dissuaded. They traveled in silence and climbed into a tall tree when night fell.

"I'll keep watch," Waxwing said. "You sleep."

"Wake me when the moon rises," Seven said. "I'll watch, and you can rest. You're still worn out from your run."

As she settled in to the crook of the tree, Seven thought again about Typhoo, Runner, and Greyson. The city seemed like a lifetime ago. Could Greyson possibly have fought off the dog? Thinking of Runner and Typhoo made her heart ache. She didn't know if they had even escaped the church, and if they did, would they be able to join her at the Notch? Could she make it so the Notch was there for them, if the time ever came?

Seven looked at the stars. "I'll find you, Mama," she promised silently. "I'll save the Notch, and bring you and

Typhoo there."

To do that, however, she would have to survive the coyote. Her eyelids drooped. Soon she was asleep. Then she dreamed.

Lucius and Isabelle were curled up on their couch with Arnica and Bobby, but there was no room on the couch for her. Instead, she went to the kitchen. In the center of the room sat a raccoon a little larger than she was, but Seven sensed instantly that she was very, very old.

She turned to leave, but the other raccoon said, "Stay, daughter."

In the dream, Seven turned back and stared. The raccoon was not Runner Moon, but Seven felt she knew her from somewhere. "You—you're First Raccoon, aren't you?"

"Very good," said First Raccoon with a warm chitter. "The Moon family has always been clever. But now you are afraid."

"The coyote is coming," Seven said. "I

have no Lucius to help me, or people to intervene. I can't possibly beat him in a fight. I don't know what to do."

"What is most important?" First Raccoon asked.

"Surviving," Seven answered simply.

"But why survive? You know that raccoons who die bravely come to me at the Great River. You know that you will come to me there."

"I am honored," Seven said. "But not yet. Not yet. My family needs me."

"And you need them."

"That's what we all need," Seven said, suddenly realizing what she must do.

The First Raccoon nodded her approval. "You shall be one of my most treasured companions, Seven-Rings Moon," she said. "But you are right. Your time to join me is not now. Because now, you know what to do."

With a jolt, Seven woke up.

Chapter 24

The progress up the mountain was slow, partly because of Waxwing. He was tired from his long journey, and the steepness of the slopes was hard for him. "I'm sorry," he said when he stopped, panting. "I meant to protect you, but I'm just putting you in danger."

Seven rubbed her head on his side. "Don't apologize," she said.

He sat up wearily and stared up the mountain. Juniper was scouting up ahead. "But you already knew about the coyote," he said.

"You couldn't have known that," she said.

As they climbed, she told him the story of the pike. His eyes grew larger as she spoke. "I've never seen such a creature!" he exclaimed. "You were so brave!"

She shook her head. "He had Arnica. I didn't have time to be scared."

Gradually, the trees gave way to shrubs, and Juniper rejoined them on the ground. By sunset, they were crossing bare rock and gravel. The wind picked up. Juniper shivered, but didn't complain. Neither did Waxwing, although Seven-Rings knew that he was worn out. She spotted some rocks, and steered her friends toward them. Gratefully, Juniper and Waxwing huddled together, relieved that the wind no longer whistled in their ears and tousled their fur.

"Stay here," said Seven-Rings. "I'll look for something to eat." She scratched between the rocks and found moss, as well as a few beetles, worms, and wood lice, which made for a meager meal even for a single creature. She brought everything back and gave most of her portion to Waxwing. Juniper did too. Although he tried to object, they insisted that he needed to rebuild his strength. He ate gratefully, and the three of them sat in silence, waiting for the inevitable.

Waxwing coughed on a bit of beetle shell. "I will fight with you," he said.

Seven shook her head. "No. I will face him by myself."

Juniper said softly, "You don't need to wait. He's right over there."

Chapter 25

The coyote stood at the edge of the rocky area, nose raised. They were downwind of him and held very still and silent. Seven thought that all the coyote needed was to listen for her rapid heartbeat. She shook herself hard. The coyote heard her, and his head snapped around. Waxwing and Juniper gasped. Seven-Rings stepped out from behind the rock.

The coyote howled, the sound ringing against the darkening sky. Seven laid her ears back. "I found you!" cried the coyote.

Seven said coolly, "I knew you were coming. You made no secret of it."

The coyote grinned wolfishly. "I figured you would be scared," he said. "Scared because you don't have your dog with you anymore." He began to stalk slowly toward Seven. "You are just a raccoon, like any other raccoon."

She sat up on her hind legs. "Well, I don't think I'd say that," Seven said. "I'm sure you've heard the stories."

"Stories from the birds? They are twittering fools. They'll say anything that suits them." He lowered his head. His eyes were bright with the excitement of the hunt.

Controlling her instinct to bolt, she continued speaking calmly. "I don't think all birds are twittering fools. Some are quite sensible."

"I don't care what you think. You made it possible for the big black dog to catch me. He made me swear the canines' strongest oath. You ruined it for me!"

"Ruined what? The chance to catch human pets, creatures that can't even find their own food?" She sneezed derisively. "That's like hunting flowers."

"They feared me! It is time for you to pay for what you did."

With a growl, he lunged for Seven. She ducked to the left, and the coyote rushed past. She whirled. The coyote skidded on the rocky ground, and, with effort, turned around to face her.

"Lucky!" he snarled, and lunged again. Seven jumped straight up into the air. Her adversary roared past, and Seven landed awkwardly. Pain shot up her foreleg, and she spun around less quickly than before. She hoped the coyote did not see her flinch, or notice that she was holding her paw off the ground. "You are not hunting as you are supposed to," she said. "You are living off of humans."

"So are you, thief," the coyote retorted. He snapped at her again, and she rolled and dodged.

"That's true," Seven admitted. "I am trying to change that. I want to find the Notch, where I can live free and wild." She kept talking as they circled each other. "We can live in the way we were supposed to live—to live wild, like First Coyote."

"Don't you dare speak that name," the coyote said.

"We need to live free of humans, to live wild," Seven persisted. Her leg throbbed.

"I live wild!" the coyote said defensively.

"No, you don't," Seven said. "You should be hunting wild prey with your pack, not pets by yourself!"

"You know nothing!" snarled the coyote, narrowing his eyes.

But Seven saw the pain there. "You lost your family, didn't you?" Rain began falling in earnest. Seven saw the coyote's true colors as if the water had washed away his tough exterior. The coyote was lost and frightened, and alone. Far more alone than she had ever been.

She sat on her haunches. "I am so sorry," Seven said, no longer afraid.

The coyote raised his head. The two stood for a moment in silence. Then the coyote began to speak, so softly that Seven had to strain to hear him over the wind. "My sire died without naming a new pack leader. The pack was divided, but most of them wanted me to be the leader. My brother knew this. He drove me out." He paused. "I should have stayed. I should have fought for what was rightfully mine. But I didn't want to die."

Seven said, "No one wants to die." For an instant, she thought of Sprucewood.

"I should have fought."

"You might have died."

The coyote stood still. The wind blew up and ruffled his fur.

"You can change," she said softly. "You hunted those pets because you were desperate. Because you need your family with you to hunt well. To be what you really are, you need to go home."

The coyote looked into Seven's eyes. "I could have killed you," he said. "But you weren't afraid. Ever."

Seven shook her head. "I was terrified. You are a mighty hunter. But I couldn't keep running. I want to live in peace, even with you." She dropped to all fours. "I'm leaving now."

The fury and hate that had burned in the coyote's eyes were gone. "You have given me much to think about," he said. "Thank you."

Seven nodded and turned away from him, walking to the stone where Waxwing and Jupiter huddled. "Let's go," she said. Speechless, they followed her out onto the rocky ground.

After watching them go, the coyote turned and headed west, back to the land of his birth.

And in the land near the Great River, First Raccoon nodded with satisfaction.

Chapter 26

The rocky top of the mountain gave way to trees once again as they climbed down the far side. Seven walked gingerly on her sprained paw, but she found a willow tree and chewed some bark. The pain eased. At her urging, Waxwing tried some, too. "Amazing," he said a few minutes later, after the bark had taken effect. "How do you know these things?"

"I listen," she said. Her eyes sparkled as she said it.

Juniper scampered down from the top of the willow. "The coyote is heading away from us, moving west," she reported.

"Sounds like he's going home," Seven said.

"But, there's something else moving," the squirrel said. "It seems to be tracking us, because it's moving in a straight line along our path."

Waxwing groaned. Seven asked, "What do you think

it is, Juniper?"

"I can't tell. It's too far off yet."

Their pace was faster now that Waxwing felt better, but it was not as quick as Seven would have liked, even with her tender paw. Juniper remained in the trees, leaping forward and looking back. After a half hour, the squirrel skidded down the tree and landed with a thump in front of the raccoons. "It's got two heads!" she said, her eyes wide.

Seven and Waxwing looked at each other in alarm. "Are you sure?" he asked.

Juniper nodded. "I could see it plainly against the sky. I counted four ears. I've never seen anything like it. And it's running!"

"Could it be a deer or something with short horns?" Waxwing asked.

Juniper shook her head.

"And you're sure it's after us?"

Juniper rolled her eyes. "If it isn't following us, that would be a huge coincidence, don't you think? It will be here before you know it."

Seven ordered, "You two go on ahead. I'll deal with this." Waxwing and Juniper hurried ahead, taking cover beneath the low-hanging branches of a blue spruce.

Within a few minutes, the creature appeared around a curve in the trail. It did have two heads—and familiar faces. "Bobby! Arni!" Seven squealed.

"Seven!" Bobby and Arnica exclaimed as one. Arnica leaped from her perch on the big bobcat's back and tackled her sister. Juniper and Waxwing peeked out from below the spruce branches, clearly confused. "Come here!" Seven called to them. "This is my sister and our friend, Bobby!" Holding on to Arnica, Seven asked Bobby, "How? Why?"

Bobby said, "I watched the coyote while he stayed with us, and he was determined to catch you. For some reason, he seemed to blame you for everything from the color of the sky to the car that hit him," he finished dryly. "I knew that wherever Colin released him, that coyote would turn his nose to the north."

"How would he know to go north?"

Bobby's whiskers drooped. "Evangeline, the red fox, had been moved to an outside run. One night I found her telling him all about the Notch."

Seven shook her head. "I can't believe she would tell him," she said.

"I don't think she meant harm, Seven," Bobby said. "Anyway, after that, I knew that it was just a matter of time before he would be released and on his way to find you. So Arnica and I discussed it. We decided we had to find you. We watched and waited and slipped away from the center. We wanted to help you." The cat licked one big paw. "But judging from the scent-story on the mountaintop, you didn't need help."

"Well, I wouldn't say that." She hugged Arnica tightly. Seven realized that her sister had grown and gained some weight. Although she wasn't Seven's equal in size, she was not as frail as she had seemed before.

Arnica looked into her sister's face and said, "Let's go home."

Seven's heart sank. "Arni, I can't go back to the center," she said.

Arnica shook her head. "Not the center—the Notch."

Bobby nodded. "Yep. We found you, and we're not letting you out of our sight ever again."

As the five friends traveled further north, the landscape grew steadily wilder. They saw fewer and fewer humans, although roads were, as always, everywhere. The roar of a truck still made Seven's heart beat faster.

One morning, their path led along the bottom of a narrow valley that had a river running and tumbling over rocks. Above them, they could hear an occasional vehicle driving along a paved highway, but there was far less traffic than they had encountered previously.

"That's a good sign, isn't it?" Juniper asked. "I mean, there aren't people in the Notch, right?"

Seven was quiet.

"Seven?" Juniper asked.

"I've been told that people are trying to build in the Notch. They want to destroy the old trees and build there."

Her news silenced all of them for a moment.

"What are you going to do?" Bobby asked.

"I have to stop them."

"How?" asked Waxwing.

"I don't know, exactly."

"It's cold," Arnica said.

Waxwing agreed. "It's much colder than back in the grove," he said.

Bobby nudged Arnica with his nose. "Come now, hop on. You've walked far enough for one day. Time for a ride." Gratefully, the little raccoon climbed up his leg and nestled onto his back.

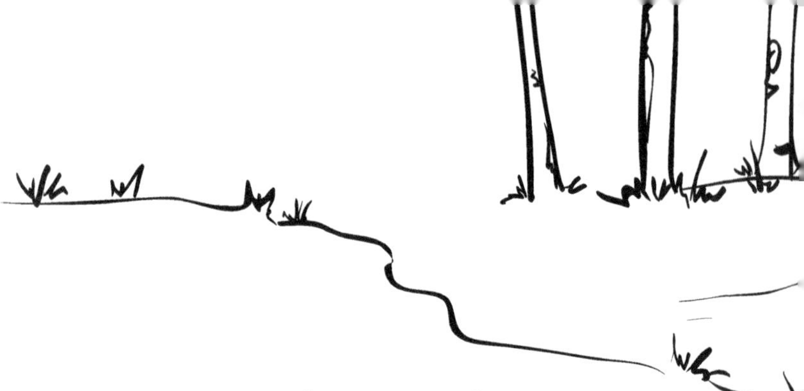

Chapter 27

That night, the travelers slept beneath a bridge. Seven and Waxwing caught minnows for supper. Juniper went searching for berries.

One by one, the animals fell asleep. Arnica was snuggled against the bobcat's side, snoring lightly. Juniper slept on one of the bridge supports above. Waxwing settled into a spot near the water's edge, his tail covering his mask and nose. Only Seven and Bobby were still awake.

"Tell me, how did you come to travel with a strange squirrel and another raccoon?" Bobby said, softly.

Seven told him about Sprucewood, and about Buckeye and Chokecherry. She told him how Waxwing came to warn her, and how Juniper decided to join her. He listened without interrupting. He shook his head. "Much has happened since you left the center," he observed.

"I was surprised at the life those other raccoons led," she said. "It was so different from what I knew. My mother was kind and took care of us. But in Waxwing's family . . ." She left her sentence hanging in the air, unfinished.

"This Corm sounds like a good sort," Bobby said.

"I just wish that things hadn't happened that way." She shuddered as she remembered the roaring engine and Sprucewood's body.

"Well, wishing won't make it so," the cat said. He stretched his forelegs, without disturbing Arnica. "I believe everything happens just as it is supposed to."

"That must be comforting."

"Especially when things seem to go wrong." They sat in silence for a while, listening to the water swirl downstream and the occasional vehicle thump over the bridge's metal plates. "How far do you plan on going?" Bobby asked.

The question caught Seven unprepared. "As far as it takes, I suppose. I feel that I will know the Notch when I see it." She studied her paws for a moment. "Does that sound foolish?"

The cat replied, "No more foolish than anything else I've ever heard. Now, we should sleep. Dawn will be here soon enough." With that, he closed his eyes and rested his head on his forepaws.

Seven resisted the urge to snuggle, instead curling up close to the cat's reassuring bulk. But she could not sleep, and finally she rose, moved away from Bobby, and sat at the water's edge. Fish peered up at her in their nearsighted way, decided she was uninteresting, and swam off. As the sky turned from black to the gray of dawn, the water's surface reflected a smaller face next to hers.

"You're awake early," Juniper said. "Bad dreams?"

Seven shrugged.

The squirrel said, "My mother's sister said that dreams tell us what the future holds. Of course, my mother said that her sister's head was as full of feathers as a bird's nest. But one time I told her one of my dreams, and it came true within a week."

Although she didn't want to know, Seven asked, "What did you dream?"

"My cousin Birch. A loud bang. Then him falling out of the tree."

"What happened?"

"He was shot by a hunter." Juniper paused. "The last time I saw him the hunter was carrying his body away by the tail." She rubbed her nose with her foreleg. Quietly, she said, "I don't like to dream." After a moment, and a sniff, Juniper said, "So, what was your dream about?"

Seven said, "Every time I tried to eat a fish, it turned into an acorn!"

Juniper responded, "For a squirrel, that's a dream, not a nightmare!"

Their laughter woke the others, who stretched and yawned and agreed that it would be good to move on before

breakfast. Waxwing shook his head as they walked, saying, "I dreamed about thunderstorms all last night."

Bobby said, "Sleeping under a bridge will do that to you."

His comment prompted Juniper to say, "Seven and I were talking about dreams, too. I had an auntie who believed they tell the future."

Waxwing replied, "Only humans are silly enough to worry about what might happen seasons from now."

"Oh, I don't know about that, Waxwing," said Seven. "Didn't you and Corm worry about what would happen if the coyote caught up with me?"

"I think it's fine to be aware of the future," said Juniper, unaware of Waxwing's discomfort. "After all, if you aren't, you're going to starve when winter comes." The others agreed.

"But there's a fine line between worrying and planning," said Seven. She glanced at her sister, in her usual place on Bobby's back. Sometimes she envied Arnica for being able to live only in the here and now, and sometimes, she felt bad for her.

They picked their way across the shallow river, stepping from stone to stone. Juniper accidentally hopped upon a turtle, and it was impossible to say who was more frightened, her or the annoyed reptile. "No reshpeckt! No reshpeckt!" crabbed the turtle, his fright making his anger more pronounced. "What do you tink you are do-ink?"

"Sorry, Grandfather," replied Waxwing. He used his most courtly manners to soothe the turtle's ruffled dignity. "My friend made a mistake, and she is most apologetic."

"Mishtake? Mishtakes come of moving too fasht. You tell your friend to shlow down."

"I will, sir, I will." Bowing over and over, he backed away as the turtle withdrew into his shell. Waxwing said to Juniper, "You were lucky he wasn't a snapper. They'll eat you as quick as look at you."

A look of queasiness crossed the squirrel's face. "What's a snapper look like?"

"Big, thick tails, and big, thick jaws," he said, delighting in watching the young squirrel's unease grow. "They eat whatever they can catch."

Juniper took to the safety of the trees.

Chapter 28

The days passed quickly for the little band. Each night, they curled up together, with Bobby as Arnica's dutiful guard. Watching the giant bobcat and the tiny raccoon, Seven's heart filled with joy because they seemed to complete each other.

One afternoon, they paused for a rest in the shade of a tall maple tree that was brilliant with the changing colors of autumn. Seven and Arnica marveled at the shades of gold, red, and orange.

Juniper said, "I know all about trees. My auntie told me about them."

"Is this the same auntie who said dreams tell the future?" Bobby asked dryly.

"No, she was my Ma's sister. This was my Da's. She said that the colder nights wake up the spirits inside the trees. They come out and dance on the leaves and turn them colors."

Arni whispered, "Is that true, Bobby?"

The cat shrugged. "It's as likely an explanation as any I know."

Suddenly, a striped chipmunk planted herself in front of Juniper. "Spirits? Spirits? That's a tree squirrel for you—always telling stories!"

"Hey!" Juniper objected.

"Who are you, anyway?" growled Bobby.

"This is my forest. I am Tamius Striatus Stripeback the 422nd, guard of these woods, and you are trespassing!" The chipmunk stamped her paw. "Now, get along, all of you! You're not welcome here."

Bobby said coolly, "You're awfully small to be making such demands." He unsheathed his claws.

Seven rested a paw on his shoulder, and he retracted his claws. "We're just traveling through. We don't plan to stay. But can you tell me something?"

Another foot stamp. "Address me with proper respect!"

Seven corrected herself. "Excuse me. Can you tell me something, Tamius Striatus Stripeback?"

The chipmunk added, "The 422nd."

Under his breath, Bobby said, "Come on, just let me eat her."

"No, Bobby." Seven sighed and said, "Tamius Striatus Stripeback the 422nd."

Said the chipmunk, "You keep your cat under control and the treeclimber silent, and maybe I will answer your question."

Indignant, Juniper said, "What did I do?"

Seven kept focused on the chipmunk. "Can you tell us

if we are near a place called the Notch?"

The chipmunk tilted her head. Seven realized she was a bright little creature, once you got past her bad manners. "First you tell me something," the chipmunk said at last. "What are you doing with this motley bunch? Raccoons, a squirrel, a bobcat? It makes no sense."

"These are my friends," Seven explained.

"Friends?"

"Yes. Surely you have friends back at the, er, castle, or headquarters, or wherever the rest of the chipmunks are."

Suddenly the chipmunk wailed, and great sobs wracked her body. "Just go, go, go!" she cried. Then she raced away through the fallen leaves.

"Stay here!" Seven ordered the others. She pursued the little animal. The chipmunk was fast, but she stumbled over a root and would have fallen into a deep ditch if Seven had not caught her from behind.

"Let me go!" she squealed.

"I won't, not until you tell me what is going on," Seven said in a firm voice. "What's going on, Tamius Striatus Stripeback the 422nd?"

The chipmunk sighed. "Just call me Tam. There aren't any others. Just me. I knew you were coming. I overheard the birds talking about the magic raccoon. And I was frightened. I wanted to scare you away." She looked nervous. "I am all alone. All the others are gone."

"Where did they go?"

"My father believed that he could find the Notch. He didn't think that he needed a seven-ringed raccoon to find it. I remember from the time I was born that he would disappear for days at a time, on scouting missions. A month ago, he came back all excited, claiming he'd finally found the legendary valley of First Raccoon. I told him the whole thing was silly, just a story, that such a place couldn't possibly exist. We argued, and I went out foraging. When I came back, everyone had left."

Seven did not know how to respond to that, so they sat for a moment in silence. Then Tam said, "Can I come with you?"

"If you apologize to everyone and not be so rude, I think so."

Tam nodded eagerly. "That's a small price to pay for not living alone anymore."

She was especially apologetic to Juniper: "I don't know anything about tree squirrels, or spirits," she said. "I just wanted to sound mean."

For his part, Bobby also apologized for threatening to eat Tam. He added, "You know, you never did answer Seven's question."

"I know where my father was going on his last journey," Tam said. "I'll show you."

Chapter 29

The golden and red hardwood trees gave way to the somber green of fir trees as the animals climbed higher and higher. The nights grew colder with each passing day. Around them, mountains of sheer granite overlooked a distant ribbon of highway that snaked along the valley floor.

"Are we there yet?" asked Waxwing after a day of particularly hard climbing.

Seven looked at her friends. Arnica appeared fine, but the strain of climbing for two was beginning to show on Bobby, although he would rather have died than admit that he was tired. Waxwing, who had never fully recovered from racing to find her, stopped often to rest. Even Juniper, whose life was climbing, was looking a little frayed.

Only Brangwy appeared fresh as she landed among them, her beak full of the nuts she brought every day during that week's arduous climb. The last item to drop from her beak, though, caught them all by surprise.

It was a fish.

Brangwy looked pleased with herself. "All week the poor cat has had nothing but nuts and berries," she said. "But now the Notch is close enough for me to fly into, catch a fish, and bring it to him."

Everyone brightened. "The Notch? We're close?" asked Seven eagerly.

Brangwy nodded. "Very close."

As the others chattered excitedly about the nearness of their destination, Brangwy hopped to Seven and spread her wings over Seven's head, giving them a private place to talk. "The news is not good," the crow said. "The road is larger. There are many trucks, many people. Some have climbed down into the Notch and begun marking the trees with bright pink X's. One person is in charge; he is building a big house on the ridge, overlooking the Notch, and wants to build more in the Notch itself." She shook her head sadly. "It does not look promising."

Seven glanced toward her exhausted friends. "Brangwy, if we left tonight, you and I . . ."

"We would be there before the sun, and well before the people," the crow said.

"Then let's do that. We'll tell everyone we're spending the night here, and once they're asleep, you and I will go."

The crow nodded, and they joined the rest of the group.

After eating, each member of the little group found

somewhere to curl up. Juniper built a nest of leaves high up in the branches. Bobby curled up beneath a shrub and was soon snoring. Waxwing settled into a needle-lined hollow under the low-hanging branches of a pine.

"I'll stand watch," said Tam.

"No, that's all right," Seven said. "You get some rest. You'll be seeing your family tomorrow." The chipmunk smiled and hurried off to where she had found a crack between a couple of rocks.

An hour after sunset, Brangwy appeared at Seven's side. "Ready to get going?" she said softly.

"Going where?" It was Arnica.

Seven nearly jumped out of her skin. "I thought you were asleep."

Arnica grinned. "I know you, sister, and I know when you are planning something. You're going to the Notch tonight, aren't you?"

Seven nodded, fearing the need to tell Arni once again that she had to go alone.

They were silent for a moment. Then Arnica said, "The Notch must be in trouble, then. You go tonight. I will bring the others tomorrow. We will be more help to you with a good night's sleep."

Overwhelmed with relief and joy at her sister's understanding, Seven touched her nose to Arni's. "I will see you soon," she said, in a voice thick with emotion.

"Now go," said Arnica. "I will stand watch, then wake Waxwing for a turn."

Knowing that the ones she cared about were safe, Seven followed Brangwy.

Although it was little more than a broad dirt track, there was indeed a road leading up, up toward the ridge that formed the crest of the mountain. Treads of heavy machinery cut deep tracks in the mud. A log carrier and another yellow machine were parked in a broad, cleared area. A few trees had been cut down, their stumps sticking out of the ground like amputated fingers. The smell of fuel lingered in the morning air, and no birds sang.

Quickly, Seven hurried across the chewed-up ground, through a group of trees, and out to the edge of the ridge, where she could look directly down into the Notch.

Filled with morning mist, the Notch looked more like a lake than a valley, with towering treetops appearing to be islands floating on fog. Brangwy asked, "What do you think?"

Seven replied, "Well, this isn't the view I was expecting."

Brangwy caw-cawed in amusement. "When the sun burns off the fog, you'll see; it is glorious."

The sound of a door slamming shut reached them through the morning air. Together they headed cautiously back to the clearing. Brangwy perched on a branch. "Come up here," she whispered. Seven climbed quickly and quietly to join her.

Three men were looking at a sheet of blue paper spread out on the hood of the pickup truck and held down with rocks on two corners and metal canisters on the others.

A white-winged crossbill, his feathers brilliant pink, perched nearby and bobbed his head in greeting. "I see you are interested in the builders," the songbird said.

"Can you tell us anything about them?" Seven asked.

The crossbill seemed pleased to be asked. "Oh, yes. I've been watching them. They come five days, then stop for two, and now have been back for four. I think after today they will not be here for two, again. The days they come, they look at the blue paper and drink from the metal canisters. Sometimes other people come. One man comes and shouts a lot. There is some digging, too."

"Can you tell me what they're building?" asked Seven.

"Big house. Biiiiig." He spread his wings for emphasis. "Two days ago they brought the big yellow thing. They've been planning for a long time. We birds have watched. Even the eagles are interested. They have a nest in the Notch."

"Eagles?"

The crossbill hopped back and forth. "They are the big ones, with the white heads and tails." He shuddered as he mentioned the eagles.

An idea began tickling Seven's brain. "Can you introduce me?"

He cocked his head. "Why does a fur-face want to talk to an eagle?"

"Let's just say I have a proposition."

Although a very bright bird, the crossbill didn't understand the word *proposition,* but he was too vain to let on. Instead, he said, "I can try. Follow me."

Brangwy looked pleased. "I knew you would come up with a plan."

"Well, we'll see. Keep watch, would you? And when the others arrive, tell them I'll be back as soon as I can."

Brangwy nodded.

The crossbill flew into one tree, waited for Seven to catch up, and then flew to another. They traveled that way for more than an hour.

"Wait here," said the crossbill suddenly. Seven waited. As the wait grew longer, she became worried. What if the songbird had become a meal instead of a messenger? A sudden rush of wind and the sound of wings made her jump. Behind her landed the largest bird she had ever seen. Brilliant yellow eyes glared at her over a yellow beak with a terrifying hook on the end. The eagle's head was white, its body deep brown, and his yellow feet ended in massive black claws. Seven's heart thudded against her ribs.

In a voice that reminded her of Lucius, the eagle said, "I am Welkin, eagle of the Notch. I hear you want to speak to me."

For a moment, Seven hesitated. Would such a creature agree to help with her scheme? "Yes, sir. I am Seven-Rings Moon."

"I know who you are. We've been expecting you for quite some time," Welkin said. "The fur folk are not the only ones who have prophecies." He groomed the feathers on one wing. "Land travel is very slow, isn't it?"

Surprised by the comment, Seven said, "Er, yes, it is. There have been many times I've wished I was a bird." She caught her breath. Would the eagle take this as an insult?

Instead, the giant bird clacked its beak in amusement. "I confess, I've never wished to be a land creature. But back to business. You are here because of the humans, yes?"

"Yes."

Welkin said, "My mate and I are very concerned. Eagles have been here in peace and quiet for many, many seasons. We ourselves have raised more than ten broods. But if the Notch falls, then that will end."

"I have an idea to make them stop," Seven said.

"How can you stop them?" Welkin said. "You are just a raccoon, and a young one at that—even if you do have seven black rings on your tail."

His remark caught Seven off guard. "You know?"

Welkin clacked his beak again. "Some stories, everyone knows, whether bird or beast. But tell me, what do you have in mind?"

Seven said, "A while ago, I was at a wildlife center. There, I learned that humans protect certain animals—animals they see as special. Like eagles. They don't allow building to happen where these animals live. If there were an eagle's nest where they are building, they would have to stop."

The eagle thought for a moment. "That is good news. But there is no nest there."

"We could build one," said Seven.

"Do you know how big an eagle's nest is?"

Seven confessed, "No."

"Let me show you," said the eagle. He flapped his wings, rose into the air, and grasped Seven gently around the upper forelegs. Suddenly she found herself rising above the trees. Heart pounding, she looked down at the world speeding by below her.

The land dropped away sharply, and then she realized they were over the Notch. The morning mist had burned off and now the sun had lit the steep-sided valley. The Notch was lined with trees that were taller and older than she had ever imagined trees could be. They looked like brightly colored cushions that she remembered from the church, appearing soft enough to sleep on. A clear river tumbled along the bottom of the valley, its bright waters reflecting the sunlight up into Seven's eyes. Along the sides of the river spread wide grassy banks. Despite the chill in the area

above, flowers still bloomed, as though the sunlight had been caught in a cup.

Her fear fell away. "It's marvelous!" Seven shouted above the roar of the wind. The eagle nodded, pleased at her reaction. He then angled his flight toward something massive at the top of a dead oak. He placed Seven carefully in the center and then landed gracefully next to her.

The eagle's nest was the largest animal-made thing Seven had ever seen. Across, it was ten times as wide as her body was long. It was constructed of fallen branches gathered over many years. Seven crept around, gathering information with her eyes, nose, and whiskers. Generations of eagles had used this nest, she realized. It was very old and had withstood many storms.

A cry from above signaled the arrival of the eagle's mate. She landed next to him. "Welkin, you've brought us a guest," she noted.

The eagle bobbed his head in greeting. "My dear Iolar, this is Seven-Rings Moon. She is the raccoon we've been expecting."

Iolar nodded to Seven. "I admit surprise at finding you in our nest."

"I brought her," explained the male. "She wants to build an eagle's nest. She thinks the presence of one would make the people stop building."

Iolar thought about the idea for a moment. "That makes sense. They give our kind a lot of room."

Seven asked, "Not all the nests are this big, are they? I mean, when they start?"

The male eagle said, "No. It takes years to get them this big. We have been working on this one a long time, and it was my parents' nest before it became ours."

"So even a small one would be enough. Just as long as the people know that eagles are building it."

Iolar tilted her white head. "I suppose we could do a starter nest. It would be good practice for the children, Welkin."

He nodded. "True. They will have to build their own nests eventually. We aren't giving this one up anytime soon."

Heart pounding, Seven asked, "Would you consider it?"

The eagles looked at each other. "Let us talk," said Iolar. They walked to the far edge of the nest.

As the eagles discussed the plan, Seven stared down into the Notch. She and Arnica—and Bobby, Juniper, Waxwing, and Tam—would be safe here. If only they could stop the construction of the big house, and all the others.

The eagles turned back to face her. "Building a nest will be a big job," said Iolar.

"We will need help, especially if we are to build the nest before the humans begin constructing the house," added Welkin.

Seven said, "I will help. So will my friends. The crossbill said that there should be two days when the people don't come. That will give us some time.

Chapter 30

The eagles returned Seven safely to Brangwy, who had been joined by the others. Juniper, once again, was convinced that Seven was magical. "A fur creature flying with the biggest of birds!" she exclaimed. "My auntie always said that you would never come back if one of those birds carried you in his claws."

Seven rubbed her shoulders. "I think flying is easier if you have your own wings." Then she explained the plan to her friends.

That night, after the men were gone, work began in earnest.

Welkin arrived first. He had chosen a tall tree very close to the intended site of the house that would be a plausible site for a nest.

Then Iolar arrived, bringing with her the pair's twins,

Halia and Luke. Bobby and Waxwing prowled the ground for fallen branches, while the eagles ranged further afield. Iolar placed the first few branches. "Ready to work?" she said to Seven and Arnica. She set them to a task, helping her and Welkin fit the branches together.

After depositing a branch, Halia asked, "Mother, this tree is still in leaf. How will the humans see the nest?"

Her question made all activity halt.

"That's something we hadn't considered," Waxwing said. The animals were silent.

A sudden flutter of wings made everyone turn. Brangwy cocked her head at them. "Then we must help autumn along." The crow nipped a leaf from a branch and let it drop. While the larger animals worked on the nest, the clever crow, the brave squirrel, and the determined chipmunk stripped away enough leaves so that the nest could be seen.

As the moon reached its peak, Seven realized that the branches were beginning to look like a nest. Arni hummed happily as her quick paws wove and tucked sticks. "Are you sure you aren't a very small eagle?" Welkin asked her, and she beamed with delight.

A branch above them quivered, and Juniper and Tam suddenly huddled against Seven, shaking with fear. Seven looked up to see a great horned owl sitting above them.

"Evening, Welkin, Iolar. What are you doing?" the owl

asked directly, as great horned owls tend to do.

"Building a nest, by which we hope to stop the big house," Iolar answered.

The owl said, "A clever idea." He looked at the crew of helpers. "You have help?"

"This is Seven-Rings Moon, her sister Arnica, and their friends. The nest was their idea, Titigli," Welkin said.

The owl shrugged. "So they're not prey. Understood."

"Want to help?" said Arnica. She held a stick up toward the owl.

Titigli chuckled. "How can I refuse an invitation from a heart so bold? What can I do?" They set him to work fetching more branches.

The work continued throughout the day, halting at sunset and resuming at dawn. Even the crossbill and the other songbirds in the area began bringing twigs and dropping them for Arnica, Tam, and Juniper.

After two days, a convincing, if rather small, eagles' nest overlooked the construction site.

Despite the fine job Brangwy, Juniper, and Tam had done of pruning the leaves, the men did not notice at first. Arni said, "Seven, what do we do if they don't see it?"

Welkin winked at the tiny raccoon. "They won't be able to miss it. Watch this." He took off, circled the site, and disappeared. When they saw him again, he was carrying a large branch and flying low and fast toward the men.

"Holy cow, look out!" cried one of the men.

"What the . . ." cried another man. Welkin zoomed over their heads and up into the unfinished nest.

"Hey, look!" said the third man.

"Since when is there an eagle's nest up here?" said the first man. The three of them stood, dumbfounded. Welkin regarded them coolly.

"Hoo boy, Larry's gonna be upset!"

One man took out his cell phone. "No signal. Must be the weather. Let's drive down the mountain."

The foreman shook his head. "I could swear that thing wasn't here Friday."

"Eagles don't build nests over the weekend," said another man.

Seven whispered to Arnica, "Not without the help of raccoons, owls, crows, bobcats, chipmunks, songbirds, and squirrels!"

Over the next several days, a stream of people arrived to see the eagle's nest. Each night, the animals worked on it, and during the day, Welkin and Iolar made a show of adding to it. The man who was building the house and planning the other houses was furious when a woman in a green uniform told him he had to stop building.

"You listen to me," he said. "I've jumped through every hoop this one-horse town has thrown in front of me. I've spent thousands—hundreds of thousands!—on fees and permits and environmental impact studies. I did everything you asked me!" His face began to turn as red as a ripe strawberry.

The woman in the green uniform tilted her chin upward. "I understand, Mr. Hollenbeck."

"This house site is no danger to the eagles! Their nest is miles away!"

The woman struggled to maintain her professional manner, and her patience. In their hiding place, the animals could sense the rise in her body temperature. "*Mister* Hollenbeck," she said, a bit louder than before. "This nest would be in your living room if you continue to build. We can't allow this project to continue."

"I've spent millions!" the man shouted.

The woman fixed him with a glare. "Maybe you should have spent a little less on your architect and a little more on your biological survey."

"There were no eagles here!" the man sputtered. "There's something going on!"

The foreman, who had been listening to the exchange, whispered to the other men, "Right, the treehuggers came and built the nest. And they released trained eagles, too!"

The men tried to hide their chuckles, but Larry Hollenbeck could hear them. "I don't care what you say!" he shouted. "That nest isn't real! I'll show you all! I will have my house, and the rest of Hollenbeck Heights!"

The other humans looked at him curiously. He climbed into his silver SUV and slammed the door. He stomped on the gas, and the tires spun, spitting rocks and dirt. Bouncing along the ruts, he departed.

The woman in the green uniform watched him go. She said to the three men, "I hoped he'd take it better than that. He knows the rules."

The foreman said, "Better watch yourself, Karen. Folks like him get mean when they don't get their way."

The woman climbed into her brown truck and turned around to drive back down the mountain.

Shaking their heads, the three men cleared out. First, the yellow construction machine rumbled away. The log carrier and the pickup truck soon followed.

Silence fell. After a few moments, Tam said, "We did it!"

They celebrated until the sun set. Welkin and Iolar departed for their real nest. The others decided to stay at the abandoned home site and travel into the Notch the next morning. Seven said playfully, "I'm going to pretend one more time that I'm an eagle." She scampered up the tree into the nest. Brangwy beat her to the top.

"You did it, Seven," Brangwy said.

"It's been a long journey," Seven replied. She looked out over the Notch, and at the river of stars that stretched overhead.

"It seems like we met a long time ago," Brangwy said. "You have changed much."

Seven shrugged. "I don't think so," she said.

Brangwy preened her left wing. "Are you sure?"

Seven paused, considering. It had been a long journey. She had seen things Runner had never known of. Runner—she sighed.

"What is it?"

"I only wish my mother and brother were here."

Brangwy brightened. "I can try to find them and tell them that you found the Notch. It is the least I can do for a magic raccoon."

With a flutter of wings, Brangwy lifted off and turned south. As Seven watched her go, Waxwing appeared over the edge of the nest. "That was amazing," he said. "I didn't think humans stopped for anything."

"They have rules, just like we do. They try to follow them," Seven said. "I used to think all of them were bad. But the people at the center were kind, and the woman in the green uniform told the angry man he had to stop building. I guess some of them are on our side."

He cleared his throat. "Look, before anybody interrupts us, I've been wanting to ask you something."

Seven cocked her ears. "Did you hear that?"

"Seven, listen . . ."

"I'm listening," she said, crawling to the edge of the

nest. "Look, isn't that the angry man?"

Sighing, Waxwing crawled to the edge, too. "Why is he here now?"

"I don't understand," Seven said. "I thought it was over."

From their vantage point in the tree, the raccoons watched Larry Hollenbeck get out and go around to the back of his SUV, from which he removed a bundle of straps. In the light of the SUV's liftgate, he put the harness on his body, fumbling a little.

"What is he doing?" Seven asked.

Waxwing replied, "I saw people use something like that once. It helps them climb like squirrels!"

After checking the straps, Larry Hollenbeck removed a crowbar from his truck and tucked it through his belt loop.

Her mind leaped forward. "Waxwing! He wants to destroy the nest," she said. "Then he can keep building."

"Lucky the eagles aren't here."

"But we can't let him destroy the nest! We'll be back where we started!"

"Let's go," said Waxwing.

"No," said Seven. "I've got to protect the nest."

"Seven, this isn't even a real nest!" Waxwing said. "It was a sham to fool the humans. We're in danger!"

"He's looking for eagles, not raccoons," she said.

"Seven, for once, think about us, will you?"

He caught her by surprise. "What do you mean?"

Waxwing spoke fast, as if he'd never get the chance again. "Seven-Rings Moon, I want you to be my mate. I want us to have kits and grow old together! If anything happens to you . . ." he stopped.

She placed a paw on his face. "I know," she said. "I feel the same way about you. But nothing is going to happen to me. I am going to protect this nest and save the Notch."

Waxwing hesitated, then nodded. "Then I will help you."

Below, the man used a special strap to attach himself to the tree trunk. Pressing themselves flat in the nest, Seven and Waxwing listened intently to his movements. They heard his boots scraping the trunk, sending a shower of bark to the ground. Slowly, the clinking of the harness hardware grew louder, as did the sound of the man's breathing.

The sounds of climbing stopped. A loud click followed; he had unhooked the strap that held him to the trunk. Scrape, scrape, scrape—he moved away from the trunk of the tree. And all the while, he panted with effort.

"On my signal," Seven whispered.

The raccoons saw the man's eyes, squinting with the effort of seeing in the night.

"Now!" said Seven. Hissing, they jumped to their feet, fur bushed out, and teeth bared.

The man howled with fright. He stepped back, but

there was nothing but air below him. He grabbed for the edge of the nest, but missed. The harness caught him. He swung from side to side. The crowbar landed on the ground with a soft thud.

Seven and Waxwing scampered down the tree, joining the others who were ranged around its base, staring up at the man, who was struggling unsuccessfully to reach a branch and right himself. "What happened?" asked Arni, rubbing her eyes.

Seven said, "He was going to destroy the nest."

Bobby licked a paw and said wryly, "I think he's stuck."

Juniper added, "I know climbing, and that's not how you do it."

Sudden flashes of red and blue lights made the animals scamper back into the undergrowth. Three vehicles pulled into the clearing. Out of the first climbed the woman in green. Out of the others climbed the sheriff and her deputies.

"Mr. Hollenbeck," called the sheriff. "It's a bit late for tree climbing." She bent down and picked up the crowbar. "Seems like you were thinking about doing some demolition work."

From up in the tree, the man declared, "I want a lawyer."

The sheriff turned to her men. "Get your gear on and get the nut out of the tree, would you?"

As the deputies put on climbing gear, the sheriff asked, "How did you know he'd come back?"

The game warden shrugged. "Just a feeling. Some people don't take no for an answer."

The sheriff stared up at the eagle's nest. "Don't you

think it's weird, I mean, that there's a nest here now? There's never been eagles on this side of the valley."

The warden shrugged. "Nature's amazing, that's all I know."

And Seven and her friends relaxed, knowing the threat was over.

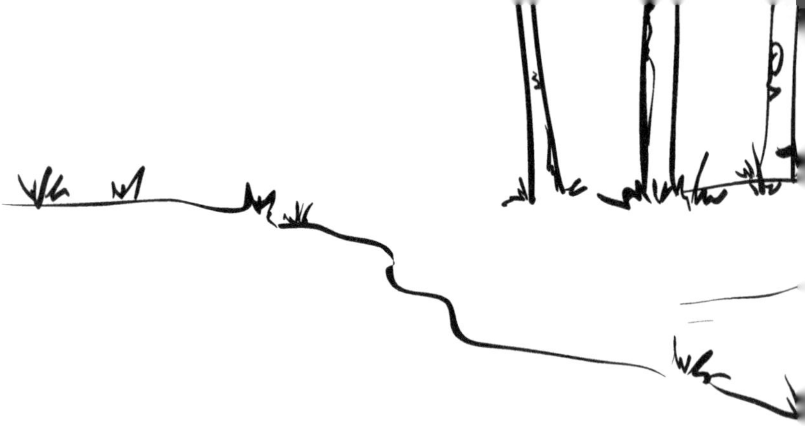

Chapter 31

Seven and Waxwing led the procession along the paths as the animals headed for the Notch. Before the morning was half gone, they stood on the ridge and looked down at the tall, ancient trees that covered the steep slopes. Here and there among the brightly colored hardwoods stood a deep green pine or spruce. They could hear the gurgling of springs, and the water ran down through the leaf litter to join a cold river that snaked along the bottom of the valley.

"We did it," Seven breathed. "We made it to the Notch."

A flutter of wings made them look up. It was the crossbill. "So what are you waiting for?"

Seven looked at Bobby, who said, "Last one down is a cranky coyote."

Whooping with delight, Bobby, Seven, Waxwing, Tam, and Juniper launched themselves off the ridge. The animals bounded down the steep slope. Sometimes they lost their footing and rolled head over tail downward, before a bit of greenery arrested their slide. Yet the falls did not dampen their spirits. Arnica, clinging to the ever-surefooted Bobby's back, chirruped with delight.

After one particularly spectacular tumble, Seven opened her eyes to see a chipmunk face peering at her. "You got here quick, Tam."

The chipmunk said, "Tam? You know my Tam?"

"Papa!" squealed Tam, skidding down the slope in her eagerness to reach the male chipmunk who had found Seven-Rings.

"Tam! My Tam!"

Seven stood up and shook herself. Soon a crowd of chipmunks surrounded them. Tam's father, Aarde, said, "We heard that the Notch was safe! An eagle's nest stopped the humans from building their big house."

"We stopped them, Papa," Tam said. "This is Seven-Rings. She came up with the idea, she convinced the eagles to help, and she kept the man from destroying it!"

A scrambling announced Juniper's arrival. "She flew with an eagle," the squirrel added for good measure.

A hush fell over the chipmunks as they stared at Seven. She grew uncomfortable at their stares. Then Aarde bowed, and suddenly every chipmunk followed suit. "You have our thanks, and our eternal loyalty," Aarde said, his voice serious.

"She's a magic raccoon," Juniper chirped. "She's done lots of amazing things!"

"Oh, Juniper, you exaggerate," Seven said.

Waxwing took her paw. "You are too modest, Seven-Rings Moon. You've made a difference wherever you've gone. You saved my family."

"You saved that coyote from himself," added Bobby.

"You got us across the big water, remember?" said Arnica, climbing down from Bobby's back.

"I remember," she said. She took her sister's paw in her own. "But there was something I wanted to do that I couldn't," she said. Regret welled up in her throat. "I couldn't save our home, or Mama or Typhoo. Arnica, I'm so sorry."

Arnica gazed up at her sister with love and pride. "You did what Mama wanted, Seven. You took care of me. And I think Mama's still alive. So is our brother. I dreamed it was true."

"And you know what my mother's sister said about dreams. . . ." said Juniper.

Seven and her friends groaned.

"What? What did I say?" asked Juniper.

Aarde took her paw. "Come with us. We have a fine colony at the base of the slope, with enough food for everyone." He looked at Bobby.

The big cat waved his paws. "Don't worry. From this point on, fish is fine for me."

With that, the travelers continued down the slope into their new home.

End Notes

Seven-Rings Moon, Arnica, Runner, Typhoo, Greyson, Waxwing, Corm, and Sprucewood are raccoons, *Procyon lotor.* Common in North America, raccoons are highly adaptable creatures, able to survive in almost any habitat. They are found from southern Canada to northern South America. They have clever forepaws, distinctive black masks, and four to ten black rings on their tails. A raccoon's tail is between 7 and 19 inches long—about half of the animal's total body length. The smallest raccoons weigh about 4 pounds and the largest about 23 pounds, but the average is 13 to 17 pounds. Males tend to be larger than females.

The rats are Norway rats, *Rattus norvegicus.* Rats are probably the world's most adaptable animal. Norway rats can gnaw through concrete and metal pipe and tread water for up to three days. They tend to live at ground level and are found in cellars and basements, as well as in sewers. They weigh between 8 ounces and 1 pound and are about 15 inches long, nose to tail.

The bats in the church are big brown bats, *Eptesicus fuscus.* These bats are often found living in city buildings; in fact, the name Eptesicus is from a Greek word that means "house flyer." The big brown bat has a wingspan of almost 13 inches, and yet weighs only about eight-tenths of an ounce—roughly the same as 20 paper clips. They eat moths, beetles, wasps, flies, and other flying insects.

Fig is a striped skunk, *Mephitis mephitis,* a member of the weasel family. Skunks are among the world's most odiferous animals, but their spray is used strictly for defense. They are preyed on by great horned owls and red-tailed hawks. About the size of a house cat, skunks usually weigh about 7 pounds. Skunks are omnivores, eating fruits, nuts, grains, eggs, meat, and even bees, which they will bat down out of the air to catch and eat. Though their eyesight is poor, their hearing is good.

Merriweather is a barred owl, *Strix varia.* Unlike most species of owls, barred owls are often active during the day. A barred owl's wingspan is roughly 3 1/2 feet. A female weighs about 2 pounds and is a little larger than a male. Barred owls eat small mammals, reptiles, and amphibians, and will even wade in water to catch fish.

Isabelle is a domestic cat, *Felis catus.* Descended from the wild cats of Africa, domestic cats have lived with human beings for about 5,000 years. Selective breeding hasn't resulted in quite so much variety as it has among dogs (see Lucius, below), but today's domestic cat comes in many sizes and fur types—including hairless.

Brangwy is an American crow, Corvus brachyrhynchos. These large, noisy birds are common throughout the United States. They are very social and sometimes form flocks of millions of birds. Scientists have found that crows are very smart and able to solve problems.

Lucius is a domestic dog, *Canis lupus familiaris.* Humans first domesticated the dog about 10,000 years ago, and today there is a dazzling variety of breeds of all shapes, sizes, and colors. Lucius is a Newfoundland ("Newfie"), a giant breed that may be more than 2 feet tall and weigh up to 150 pounds. The Newfie loves the water; it even has webbed feet.

The coyote *(Canis latrans)* is a member of the dog family. The coyote is an extremely adaptable animal and has expanded its range tremendously over the last few decades. Although they, like all dog family members, are primarily meat eaters, they can and do eat many other things, including fruits, vegetables, insects, household trash, and carrion. Coyotes weigh between 15 to 46 pounds and are about 30 to 40 inches long, making them much smaller than wolves and much larger than foxes.

Bobby is a bobcat, *Lynx rufus.* Bobcats are found from Canada to Mexico, although they are shy and hard to spot. They weigh between 9 to 33 pounds and are 25 to 40 inches long, including their short tails, which are only 4 to 7 inches. As a carnivore, a bobcat eats mostly rodents, rabbits, and large ground birds.

Buckeye, Chokecherry, and Juniper and her sisters are gray squirrels, *Sciurus carolinensis.* These tree acrobats faced extinction after the land was cleared for farming. However, the planting of trees in cities and suburbs gave the gray squirrel a new lease on life, and it is now common. Gray squirrels are medium-sized squirrels, weighing between 12 and 26 ounces. They are between 15 to 21 inches long, including a tail that is 6 to 10 inches long.

Tam, Aarde, and their family members are eastern chipmunks, *Tamius striatus.* These little creatures are members of the squirrel family. Weighing almost 5 ounces, they are among the largest chipmunks and have five black stripes on their backs. At full growth, they are about 10 inches long. They usually live alone.

Welkin, Iolar, and their children are bald eagles, *Haliaeetus leucocephalus* Their wingspans can reach 7 1/2 feet, and the birds weigh about 7 pounds. They eat mostly fish, but will also take small mammals and eat carrion.

Titigli is a great horned owl, Bubo virginianus, which range from Canada to the tip of South America. With a wingspan of about 4 1/2 feet, they weigh about 3 pounds. They catch skunks, mice, rats, woodchucks, rabbits, and other birds, including turkeys and geese. The name Titigli means "great horned owl" in the language of the Mi'kmaq, a North American Indian tribe. It is pronounced "dii·di·gê·li."